SHOULD HAVE PLAYED POKER

To Jeane –
A woman who shows
determination every time
she plays a hand. Please enjoy
my version of Mah jongg and mystery –

Deb H. Goldt

A CARRIE MARTIN AND THE MAH JONGG
PLAYERS MYSTERY

SHOULD HAVE
PLAYED POKER

DEBRA H. GOLDSTEIN

FIVE STAR
A part of Gale, Cengage Learning

GALE
CENGAGE Learning·

Farmington Hills, Mich • San Francisco • New York • Waterville, Maine
Meriden, Conn • Mason, Ohio • Chicago

GALE
CENGAGE Learning®

LIBRARY OF CONGRESS CATALOGING-IN-PUBLICATION DATA

Names: Goldstein, Debra H., author.
Title: Should have played poker / Debra H. Goldstein.
Description: First edition. | Waterville, Maine : Five Star Publishing, [2016] | Series: A Carrie Martin and the Mah jongg players mystery
Identifiers: LCCN 2015049812| ISBN 9781432831592 (hardback) | ISBN 1432831593 (hardcover) |ISBN 9781432831530 (ebook) | ISBN 1432831534 (ebook)
Subjects: LCSH: Women lawyers—Fiction. | Family secrets—Fiction. | Murder—Investigation—Fiction. | Mah jong—Fiction. | Mystery fiction. | BISAC: FICTION / Mystery & Detective / Women Sleuths. | FICTION / Mystery & Detective / General.
Classification: LCC PS3607.O4843 S56 2016 | DDC 813/.6—dc23
LC record available at http://lccn.loc.gov/2015049812

First Edition. First Printing: April 2016
Find us on Facebook– https://www.facebook.com/FiveStarCengage
Visit our website– http://www.gale.cengage.com/fivestar/
Contact Five Star™ Publishing at FiveStar@cengage.com

Printed in the United States of America
1 2 3 4 5 6 7 20 19 18 17 16

In memory of my mother
Erica Green
who taught me about love, integrity, and resilience

ACKNOWLEDGEMENTS

Writers tend to listen to the voices in their own heads. Often, it helps to hear a more objective viewpoint. In my case, I owe great thanks to T.K. Thorne, Fran and Lee Godchaux, Lisa Sadler, and Grace Topping for willingly reading various versions of my work in progress. I'm grateful for the sound technical advice offered by Linda Rodriguez, Leslie Budewitz, and Hank Phillippi Ryan and the editorial comments that strengthened the manuscript and query from Chris Roerden, Ben Furnish, and Ramona DeFelice Long.

Two conference shout-outs must be made. The first is to the Alabama Writers Conclave for awarding a 2013 First Place Chapter Award to *Should Have Played Poker* when only the first chapter existed. Killer Nashville receives the second accolade for giving me the opportunity to have the opening pages critiqued by Demi Dietz. Her subsequent acquisition of the manuscript for Five Star, a part of Gale, Cengage Learning still has me happy dancing. Demi, Gordon Aalborg, Nivette Jackaway, Tiffany Schofield and Tracey Matthews have all contributed to making the Five Star process simple and enjoyable.

My final thoughts are for my husband, Joel, who steadfastly encourages my writing efforts and is always willing to eat out.

CHAPTER ONE

"The first time I thought of killing him, the two of us were having chicken sandwiches at that fast-food place with the oversized rubber bird anchored to its roof."

"I know the one." I hand a cup of coffee across my desk to a woman I have not seen in twenty-six years.

With her free hand, Charlotte Martin pushes back a gray strand escaping from her ponytail. "It didn't seem like the right thing to kill him in a place they close on Sundays. Besides, Carrie, being a lawyer, you can understand I didn't want to do prison time. I decided it would be better to divorce your father."

In all the ways I've imagined reconnecting with my mother, I never thought it would be on a Sunday morning in my office discussing why she once wanted to murder my father. Stunned that this blue-jeaned woman carrying a large plastic bag knew I worked at Carleton Industries or that I'd even be here today, I put my coffee down on the brief I was drafting.

Until she spoke and I had a faint recollection of the lilt of her voice, I had no idea who she was.

I rummage in my desk for a packet of sweetener, wondering why anyone, especially my mother, could ever think of killing my father, the former minister of Wahoo, Alabama's Oakwood Street Church. Rather than ask, I wait. One thing I learned before I washed myself out of the police academy to go to law school is that there's no reason to rush. You can often learn more from silence than by asking endless questions.

9

My hand trembles as I pour the last of the coffee into her mug. "So, you walked out on him instead?"

"Not quite. I went home that Saturday night promising myself I'd be a dutiful wife, but as we lay in bed with him snoring and me seething, I again felt like killing him. When I found myself debating whether to stab him, beat him with the bedside lamp, or wait until morning and poison his oatmeal, I knew I needed to leave." She chuckles, letting me see laugh lines etched into her face.

"Don't look at me like that," she says. "Little things kept getting to me. Things like the way he left his black socks next to our bed every night for me to pick up. Or, how he sprinkled as much Gold Bond powder on our bathroom floor as on him."

She leans forward in my client chair—as close as she can get into my personal space—and asks, "Have you ever had an urge to avoid doing something because you knew it might turn out wrong?"

My back stiffens as I start to pull away from her, but I consciously relax so I can peer closely at her face—looking for something familiar. "Never. I was brought up to believe that running is the coward's way."

I may have gone too far. I can't tell whether her eyes are watering or reacting to the steam rising from her coffee. Before I can apologize or soft-pedal my words, she cuts me off.

"Then you're a lucky person."

For fear of breaking our rapport, such as it is, I force myself to bite back a retort to her "lucky" comment or ask my mother why in twenty-six years she never wrote or even sent a birthday card.

"Where did you go?"

Sinking back into the chair, she visibly relaxes and picks up the thread of her story. "Reno."

"Reno? That's a far way from Alabama."

"True, but unlike Alabama, it was one of the states that allowed a no-fault divorce after living there only six weeks." She pauses to sip her coffee. "From the movie-star magazines I'd read, I thought Reno would be an interesting place to be." She stops and stares at her reflection in my office window.

"Things didn't turn out to be nearly as star studded or glamorous as the magazines painted Reno. Girls like me were a dime a dozen, but without dimes. We shared what we had. I loved being responsible only for me—until everything went horribly wrong."

I struggle to keep my face neutral. She hated caring for me? Was I so bad?

She sets her coffee mug down again. Her hands shake too much to bring it to her mouth. "I didn't go right away, you know. The night before leaving, as I weighed what to take, he stirred and reached across the bed for me. I lay down again and tried to sleep, but the thought of murdering him kept getting stronger. I was afraid I might snap and do it. I loved him and you too much to take a chance of that happening."

They say love and hate are opposite emotions existing at the same time, but something in her story doesn't feel right. One minute she tells me she hated him enough to kill him, the next she loved us. Abandoning us seems a funny way to show it.

"Couldn't you have simply talked out your issues?"

"No. He was too powerful for me. Not in a physical way," she quickly adds. "He could make anything sound logical and possible." After all the disagreements my father and I had over the proper way for a minister's daughter to behave, I can understand that point.

"That Sunday morning, when he went to give me a good-morning kiss, I turned away. I told him I thought I had picked up the bug going around and should skip church. I offered to help him get you ready, but he said, 'No need' while he tucked our comforter around me."

I don't ask, but I wonder if he tucked the comforter around her like he tucked me in when I was a kid.

"Would it have been so bad to stay?"

"Staying would have been easier."

My mother staying definitely would have been easier for me. Even at twenty-nine, I remember how many nights I cried because I wanted her instead of my father to read me my bedtime story.

Not sure what to ask next, I decide to pin down what went so "horribly wrong" in Reno. As I shotgun questions at her, she lifts her left leg almost even with the top of my desk and tugs the cuff of her jeans up a few inches, revealing a wide scar that continues as far as she can expose it. Putting her leg down, she pushes up the left sleeve of her blouse so I can see a matching scar on her arm.

"It happened the fourth week. The girls taught me that if you played nickel slots, waitresses came around with free drinks and, if you played long enough, free food. I'd gotten pretty good turning a two-dollar roll of nickels into dinner; but that night, I ran through my nickels quickly. I was walking back to my apartment when a drunk in a Cadillac hit me. I woke up a few days later with casts on my arm and leg. My memory is foggy, but seeing my husband, in his ministerial collar, sitting in a chair next to my bed is seared into my mind."

"Dad? Dad went to Reno?" I wonder if she is lying. My father always has preached to me about honesty and integrity, but in all these years, he never told me he knew where my mother was.

"Yes, when I woke, he was there. He wanted me to go home with him, but I couldn't." She leans down and begins to untwist the pipe cleaners cinching the plastic bag near her feet. "He let his insurance cover my hospital bills and made arrangements for me until I could be on my own again."

She rummages through her bag until she pulls out a well-handled envelope. Before I can ask what it is, she stands so that she is looking down at me. I stand, too. She holds the envelope out, but I keep my hands down by my sides. "It won't bite," she says, putting the envelope on a stack of file folders on my desk. "We divorced once I was back on my feet. By then the congregants had stepped in to help him and you, as I knew they would."

"But why come back now? That's what this afternoon's discussion is about, isn't it?"

"Yes." She picks up her bag. "I promised him then I would give you this. I tried to keep my promise for many years, but until now, I've never had the courage to honor it. Maybe," she says, already standing in my doorway, "when you read that letter, you'll understand what kept me from being his wife."

"Or my mother," I whisper—but she is no longer there.

She is gone from the hall before I can ask the questions now ready to flow from my tongue. Why now? Where have you been? How did you live? Did you ever have another little girl to love?

My fingers trace the sharp edges of the envelope. I start to open it, but stop, fearful its contents will prevent me from finishing my brief. There isn't time before the brief is due to dwell on apologies and might-have-beens. I put the envelope in my pocket.

As I pick up my pen, my eyes rest on the picture on my desk from my college graduation. My father and I are both smiling in the picture, unaware of the diagnosis he will receive a few years later that will change our lives forever. I decide that before I open the envelope, I owe it to my father to first seek answers from him about my mother.

CHAPTER TWO

As I duck under the banner strung across Sunshine Village's doorway, the envelope in my pocket crackles. I rest my hand on it in the same way I repeatedly did when I was working on my brief. Even though I don't feel like laughing, I am amused by the contradiction between the posted permanent "No Children" sign and the low-hanging "Children's Halloween Festival 2–4 p.m."

From its colorful lettering, I know the banner had to be made by Carolyn Holt. Since retiring from her children's librarian job at the Wahoo Library and taking a room at Sunshine Village, Carolyn delights in coming up with activities for her fellow residents and in finding ways to guilt children and grandchildren into visiting their retirement home "prisoners."

Glancing at my watch, I assume the festival is about midway through. Ordinarily, I would poke my head into the dining room to listen to my sometime-substitute mother, Carolyn, clad from head to foot in Burberry plaid, read ghost stories in the same library whisper that once scared my childhood friends and me. Today, I need to get upstairs and prompt my father to recall the time in my life I only have snapshot memories of.

I punch the elevator button. Waiting, I hear a loud wolf whistle followed by the command, "Leave Carrie alone!" I was going to avoid visiting with any resident hanging out in the lobby, but I look around to see where the whistle and comment came from. A group of poker players is sitting at a folding table crammed into an alcove near the elevator.

"Why aren't you in the card room?" I ask.

"Ms. Holt appropriated it for apple bobbing," one says. I recognize his voice as the one who instructed the wolf whistler to leave me alone. He lays his cards down declaring, "Full house." Immediately, he grabs the chips from the center of the table. Judging by the stack already in front of him, he is having a great afternoon. "Want to play a hand?" He looks down the hall in the opposite direction from the now-opening elevator doors. "I could use a little break."

"Sorry, I can't play poker now. Maybe another time." I still face the poker players as I step forward and almost collide with Sunshine Village's executive director, Barbara Balfour. Barbara nods, but I can't tell if she is acknowledging my "Hello" or the whistler's newest sound of approval. Anxious to see my father, I push the third-floor button twice.

Almost three years ago, when my father received his early-dementia diagnosis, I was so appalled by Sunshine Village's stark décor, structured movie nights, and arts-and-crafts activities, I begged him to move into my student apartment. He refused. "Honey, I know you mean well, but I need to be settled while I still can do some good. I may be giving up my formal pulpit, but a kind word or deed doesn't require remembering where I put my eyeglasses or car keys."

I couldn't admit it then, but my father was right. After he moved out of the parsonage, he definitely made a home and friends here. Happily, since his recent transfer from the fourth floor to the six-bed Alzheimer's wing on the third floor, his friends continue to visit him.

When the elevator doors open, I expect the third floor will be a silent tomb, with almost everyone in the lobby or dining room, but instead I hear "Code Blue. Room 346. Code Blue." People are running toward Room 346. I run, too. Room 346 belongs to my dear friend, and surrogate mother after mine abandoned me, Carolyn Holt.

CHAPTER THREE

People are crowded in the hall outside of Carolyn's room. I pray this is like the last time a Code Blue was called for Room 346. That day, Carolyn dropped a hearing aid under her dresser. To retrieve it, she got down on the floor and felt around for the device. An aide walking by saw Carolyn's feet sticking out in the middle of the room and pulled the emergency cord. When staff members burst into her room with a crash cart, Carolyn was sitting up, hearing aid in hand.

The expressions on the faces of those gathered outside Room 346 tell me Carolyn won't be bouncing up so quickly this time. I push my way through the crowd, but a wispy woman body-blocks me at the open doorway. I recognize her as one of the ladies who plays Mah jongg in Sunshine's card room.

"Ms. Balfour called the police," the woman informs me. "She's gone downstairs to meet them." I start to ask why the executive director called the police, but clamp my teeth together when she steps aside long enough for me to slip into the room.

Marta, my favorite third-floor nurse, is inside the room with her arms tightly wrapped around a sobbing gray-haired woman. Both are staring at a silver knife jutting from the back of the Burberry raincoat–clad body on the floor. Shocked, I force my eyes away from the silver sheath in Carolyn's coat and reach to check for a pulse. I pull back when Marta barely shakes her head at me. She draws the frail woman closer to her with one hand and makes the sign of a cross with her free hand.

Looking at the woman again, I remember she is Mrs. Schwartz, another member of the Mah jongg group. Her arrest and subsequent release last year after keying another resident's car was the talk of Sunshine Village for weeks. Somehow, I bet today's story will be talked about a lot longer!

I visually survey the room like they taught me to do at the police academy. Halloween treats are strewn on the floor next to an overturned Burberry tote. A Burberry rain hat and coat obscure the dead woman's face, but the fluorescent ceiling light makes the protruding silver knife unmistakable. I carefully sidestep the blood pooled alongside sneakered feet. Seeing how Mrs. Schwartz is shuddering, I suggest, "Marta, why don't we take Mrs. Schwartz into the hall to wait for the police?"

Years of farm chores followed by years of providing patient care have given Marta a solid muscular build, but with a gentle touch she silently guides Mrs. Schwartz from the room. I hesitate in the doorway. I don't want to leave Carolyn alone. I look around the room, but except for the body and the Halloween candy, nothing else appears to be out of place.

Nothing, except that the most alive person I have ever known is now still. I kneel to say good-bye to the woman who helped me learn to read and took me to buy my first prom dress. Not wanting to use my hand to disturb any evidence, I take my mother's envelope from my pocket and carefully raise the edge of the hat.

For a moment, I stare and hold my breath. The face before me is smooth and almost young in repose. No laugh or worry lines are apparent.

Time passes before I move, but then the ex-almost cop in me reacts. I cross the room and again use my mother's envelope to close the door and flip the lock. With my cell phone, I snap pictures of the room and the body from all angles. I can't help it. This may be the only chance I have to make my own record of the crime scene.

I shoot pictures as fast as I can. The doorknob jiggles. A male voice orders, "Open up in there." I stuff the phone back in my pocket. Using the envelope I flick the lock. As I shove the envelope into my pocket, the door is pushed open from the hallway.

A young, uniformed policeman stands there, scowling at me. Over his shoulder I see a taller, salt-and-pepper-haired man, probably his partner, and Barbara Balfour. Barbara and the older officer prevent the Mah jongg door guard from following the younger policeman into the room, but they can't stop her from yelling. "Don't expect too much from that one! Babyface is the one who arrested Hannah last year."

Hannah. Hannah Schwartz. That is the full name of the visibly shaken woman who must have found the body. From where I stand, I am pretty sure no one except me can see the hardening of the young officer's facial muscles at the mention of Hannah Schwartz's name. Even a year later, he apparently harbors bad feelings about the keying incident.

I start to leave, but Babyface blocks my exit. "What were you doing in here?"

"Officer . . ." I strain to read the name on his badge. My father always taught me to personalize a sticky situation. ". . . Robinson. It's okay. I thought it was better if Marta got Mrs. Schwartz out of here." I point to the body, and shove my other hand back into my pocket hoping Officer Robinson won't see how much my hands are shaking. My fingers brush against the envelope. "I know her. I mean, I knew her. I didn't want her to be alone."

Babyface frowns. I rush to explain a little more. "Besides, with so many people here because of the festival, I thought staying in the room would help secure the scene until you arrived." I feel my body relax as my training takes over and I focus on the procedural aspects of the crime. "It's obviously a homicide. You're going to need evidence techs, and it might be a good idea to lock down the building and find out who already signed in and out this afternoon."

"Sorry, ma'am, I didn't know you were a detective," Baby-face drawls.

"I'm not. I didn't finish the academy." He smirks as I continue. "Law school was a better fit for me, but that doesn't mean I don't remember a thing or two about what to do at a murder scene."

The two officers exchange a look between themselves. I hadn't noticed the salt-and-pepper-haired policeman enter the room. The older officer peers from the body to me. "How is it again you came to be in here?"

"My dad's room is on the other side of the nursing station. I was getting off the elevator when the Code Blue was called. I recognized the room number as Carolyn's."

Babyface reasserts his control of the situation. He begins to make a comment, but I cut him off. I refuse to give Officer Robinson the satisfaction of breaking down in front of him so I say, "Look, it doesn't take a rocket scientist to figure out this is a murder." I point at the protruding knife.

"May I speak with you over here for a moment please?" Baby-face asks, already guiding me with a firm grip on my elbow. He positions me with my back to the body. "Ma'am, we appreciate your opinions, but you need to let us do our job. I'm sure Ms. Holt would have appreciated it."

"I'm sure she still would because that's not Carolyn Holt."

CHAPTER FOUR

Babyface points a stubby finger at the body and demands, "Who is she?"

He tightens the grip of his hand still wrapped around my elbow. I pull free and rub my arm. I am about to tell him who is lying dead on the floor in Room 346, but I am drowned out by a commotion in the hall.

"It's Ms. Holt!" a woman's voice cries.

The older officer goes to the door and motions for his partner. I follow Officer Robinson as he hurries toward the nurse's station, leaving his partner to guard the room. Most of the earlier crowd has left, but an auburn-haired man and Barbara Balfour huddle near the third-floor linen closet. Rounding the desk behind Babyface, I see Carolyn lying tumbled on a pile of towels near the man's shoes. She wears underwear and Burberry boots. He has on lace-up dress shoes.

Carolyn moans. As Barbara helps her lean against the wall, the man grabs a sheet from the closet to shield her from everyone's inquisitive eyes. Babyface pulls his radio out and calls for an ambulance.

Even from a distance, I can make out a big lump on Carolyn's left temple. She is going to have a nasty bruise. Satisfied that Carolyn is being taken care of, I seize my chance to escape Babyface by going to my father's room.

The young officer with the smooth face cuts me off before I can pass the nurse's station. Taking a stance directly in front of me, he rests one hand on his holstered gun and jerks his other hand back toward Room 346. "If Ms. Holt is in the linen closet out here, who's lying in there?"

I take a breath before answering, forcing my gaze away from his fingers drumming the grip of his gun. I know I should answer him immediately, but the only thought in my head at the moment is how much he reminds me of Barney Fife on the old *Andy Griffith Show*. I wonder if the sheriff of Wahoo issues the young cop more than one bullet for his gun. Because I don't think it will improve our relationship, I refrain from asking.

"Well?"

"Yes, well?" interrupts another voice from over my shoulder. Babyface backs off. I turn to face the man behind me.

"Brian! What are you doing here?"

For a moment, we stand silently staring at one another. A blue blazer and French-cuffed pink shirt set off the hazel-flecked eyes I once loved to peer into. The spread of his jacket indicates a few pounds gained in the five years since we lived together. I glance at Detective Brian McPhillip's ringless hand and take comfort in the fact that the hours I unwillingly have been putting in at the gym every week probably have me in my most toned shape ever.

In the old days, our almost identical 6'4″ height, when I wore my favorite heels, and the contrast between his dark, Irish Catholic looks and my fair skin, blue eyes, and apple-red hair, made us a striking couple.

"So, Carrie, you know who our victim is?"

"Yes." I taste each word on my tongue. "My mother."

CHAPTER FIVE

"Okay, Carrie," Brian says. "You've got some 'splaining to do—quickly." We stand inside the doorway of Room 346. I keep my eyes on the techs working the crime scene. They pretty much fill the small room.

After the paramedics checked Carolyn out and took her to the hospital, Brian directed Babyface's partner to secure the scene around the linen closet and record the names and contact information of everyone in its vicinity. He sent Babyface downstairs to get today's guest log. Now, with everyone busy, he focuses his attention on me. "You want to tell me how we have two detectives on this case—one of whom is related to the deceased?"

"Oh, we don't," I assure him. "You're the detective."

"Thanks for the vote of confidence."

Remembering the unwritten code of ethics between fellow officers, I remain mum about any of the things Babyface or his partner did.

When Brian plays with his belt buckle, but doesn't say anything else, I nod to the 346 number above the doorway.

"My father's room is 341. I was getting off the elevator to go visit him when I heard the Code Blue for 346. Knowing 346 is Carolyn's room number, I panicked. I responded the same way you would have. I checked out what was going on."

"And?"

"And, I found one of the residents guarding the door. She

told me Barbara called the police and was waiting for them downstairs. Then, she let me slip into the room."

Seeing Brian wrinkling his forehead like he used to do when I said something he didn't quite understand, I pre-empt him. "Many of the Sunshine folks associate me with my father. You know, even now, as in and out of it as he is, a lot of the people here find him comforting."

"He always had that way about him," Brian says. I don't say anything because as close as my father and I have become as his mind has begun to fail, there were plenty of times he wasn't always the most comforting person to me. Then again, some of my choices, like going to the police academy, moving in with Brian, or just not going to church regularly, weren't exactly up to my father's standards.

Now it is my turn to get us back on topic. "I had no idea it wasn't Carolyn. The Burberry hat and coat covered everything except the knife sticking out of her back."

I pause as I recreate the scene in my head. Brian waits, so I hurry to fill the silence. "Brian, I've known Carolyn as far back as I can remember. I didn't want her to be alone." I blink my eyes and look to see how he is reacting, but I can't read him. "I wanted to get down on my knees and say good-bye or maybe mutter a prayer for my old friend. I didn't realize it wasn't Carolyn until I could see under the hat."

I am too overcome to continue talking. Brian doesn't press me. Instead he looks around the room. He is evaluating the physical setting, the body, and the overturned bag of Halloween treats much as I did earlier. I wonder if he sees something I missed.

With as much as Brian knows about me, he is probably wondering what I'm not sharing with him. I definitely don't want to tell him or anyone about my mother's envelope until I talk to my father. Hopefully, because he saw how the Burberry hat flopped across her face, he believes I couldn't see enough at first to know the woman lying on the floor of Carolyn's room *was* my mother.

"Red," he says, slipping easily back into his nickname for me, "we've only got a few more minutes. We both know you've had a non-relationship with your mother almost all of your life. When did that change?" He steps closer to me. I smell his aftershave. He still wears Brut, the one I picked out for him.

To gather my thoughts, I turn my wrist to look at my watch. I wait a moment to be sure it is working. It is. "About five hours ago."

He cocks an eyebrow and tightens his jaw, removing any sign of his dimples. "So, why did she come back today? Did you know she was your mother?"

I decide lying won't help anything, but volunteering everything, especially the envelope, would be too much enlightenment.

CHAPTER SIX

Brian empties the third-floor lounge for our use. I'm uncertain how to begin. During the two years we were together, I can't remember how many times he accused me of refusing to commit to him because I hadn't addressed my mother's abandoning me when I was three. I always replied that that issue was resolved long ago. Our problem, I would explain, was that we both needed time to find ourselves. Thinking back, I knew we were at different points in our lives—him ready for a police career and me thinking about leaving the academy, unsure of what I wanted. Truth be told, not much has changed during the intervening years.

"Until she showed up at my office this morning, I hadn't seen Charlotte Martin in twenty-six years."

"Your office?" He sweeps his hand across the front of his hair. "What made her go to Carleton Industries? How did she know you'd be there?"

"I'm not sure. I've been asking myself the same questions—especially how she knew where I worked and that I would be there today. Then again, anyone who knows me knows that, except for when I visit my father, I'm there almost nonstop seven days a week." Great, I've just told him I am a workaholic with no social life. I take my suede blazer off and carefully place it on the couch between us. "Aren't you getting warm?"

"Not particularly." He leans back against the vinyl couch. "Did you recognize her?"

26

"Not at first. When she stuck her head into my office, I really wasn't paying attention. I was working." Brian doesn't need me to paint him a picture of the sweatshop I work in. He's used to a 24/7 job. "So many people work on the weekends, it could have been anybody. I was actually a little annoyed that she'd gotten by the front-desk guard because she looked like a bag lady."

"Why didn't you get rid of her?"

I pick up a needlepointed pillow someone has left on the couch. I turn it over in my hands. One side is solid navy blue and the other has stitching that reads: "There's No Place Like Home—and This Isn't It."

"I don't know." I flip the pillow again. "I guess because she asked for me by name, and I had a feeling as she spoke that I knew her. The cadence of her voice and her laugh felt familiar."

The memory of her laugh and the warm feeling it gave me come rushing back, but I know I can't stay in that moment. If I do, I won't be able to control the tears welling up in me. Instead, I focus on Brian. "I didn't know what to do, so I offered her a cup of coffee. I hadn't even finished pouring her coffee before she told me she once thought of killing my father."

Brian bends in, closer to me. "What did you say?"

I think about the rest of our conversation, deciding which parts to share. With a shrug, I drop the pillow on top of my coat. "I clearly remember her smiling as she put her coffee down on my desk. It was surreal, and I was sort of frozen, watching every detail of what she did."

"What did she do?"

"Oh, you know." I flip my palms upward. "Things like pushing back a strand of hair that had escaped from her ponytail, blowing on her coffee to cool it, and simply staring at me. I was watching her do these little things when she told me it was better to divorce my father than do prison time."

It doesn't seem right to tell Brian that I so wanted to know why my mother had left us that I was hooked on listening to anything she said. "We discussed several ways she had considered killing my father." Brian looks surprised. "But," I assure him, "while she was describing possibilities ranging from stabbing him with a kitchen knife, hitting him over the head with a lamp, or poisoning his oatmeal, she laughed at herself. She had a lot of laugh lines etched into her face." I wonder if Brian still knows me well enough to realize how relieved I am that my mother had things to laugh about in her life, but how much I resent her failure to be around for us to laugh together.

Brian waits expectantly for me to continue, but I don't want to tell him it was the moment she laughed that I was sure who she was. It is too private. I don't remember much about how my mother looked before she left, but I have always had a faint memory of her voice and laugh.

"And then?" Brian prods.

"Then things got weird. She asked if I ever avoided an urge to do something wrong by walking away from the situation. I told her never, and underscored that running is the coward's way."

"How did she respond?"

"She said I was a lucky person."

"I understand her point."

I shoot him a look he's seen from me before, as I question whether I should even be having this conversation with him.

"Where did she go when she left your father?" Brian asks.

"Reno." He mouths surprise, but doesn't comment aloud. I repeat to him what my mother told me about the divorce law requirements in different states. "I understand the six-weeks residency requirement was important to her," I explain, "but I really think she picked Reno because the chance to see movie stars appealed to her."

"So, what brought her back now?" Maybe because Brian takes my hand or looks at me too kindly, I don't respond. Instead, I pull back, perhaps a little too quickly, but in time to keep Babyface from seeing us holding hands when he steps into the room.

I'm glad Babyface needs Brian's attention. While they talk in the corridor outside the third-floor lounge, it gives me a break to compose myself. There is not much more I want to share with Brian. I don't think it necessary to explain to him the thoughts of love and hate that went through my mind while my mother was in my office or how my mother believed staying would have been easier than the path she chose. More importantly, I don't want to tell him about the envelope.

I feel an urge to get away from Brian. Not only do I need to check if my father was okay after hearing the Code Blue but, more importantly, I want him to help me sort out my conflicting feelings about my mother so I can face reading what is in the envelope.

"Sorry about that." Brian says, sitting down again, but this time at the far end of the couch. He glances at the door. "I'm beginning to agree with you. I'm not sure Robinson is ever going to make it off the street."

"I never said . . ."

He grins. It is scary how well he still knows me, including how I react to incompetence. "Carrie, you were telling me how your mother . . . Why she came back and how she knew you'd be at your office."

"I really don't know. She was there and then she was gone."

"Well, when she left, did she indicate she was going to the retirement home? Was she going to see your father or meet someone else?" I shrug my shoulders. Brian keeps asking me questions about who might have killed her at the retirement home, but I don't have any answers for him until he asks me if I know anything else about her time in Reno.

"Yes. She was hit by a car and woke up in the hospital with her arm and leg in casts and my father sitting next to her bed."

"Your father?"

I nod. "Either she lied to me or my father has by omission. He never told me he knew where she went."

My voice quivers as I rub my forehead where I am beginning to feel a headache coming on. "She showed me her scars, one on her leg and a matching one on her arm."

"That explains her scars. The medical examiner will wonder about them."

"I need to check on my father. I don't think there is anything else I can tell you." I push the pillow aside and grab my jacket.

"Are you sure?" He leans forward staring at me, but he doesn't try to touch me again.

I step away from him as he reminds me that either he or one of the officers will need to get a formal signed statement from me later. For now, I can't stand the chance Brian will push me for what I'm not saying. Better to visit my father than tell Brian that while her mother was confessing her demons to me, she kept untwisting the pipe cleaners cinching the plastic bag she carried. It is much better for me to leave on the pretext of checking on my father than admit the sound I am positive Brian can hear when I move is my mother's unopened envelope in my pocket.

I need to know why my mother came back and to understand how, when I had just a few moments to barely get to know her again, she is gone for good. I am afraid to let Brian in too much, but I can't handle this alone. I must get to my father quickly to give him a chance to tell me what he probably would never admit if he were in his right mind.

CHAPTER SEVEN

Pushing open the door of my father's room, I pause when I hear a voice speaking so softly that I can't make out the words. Inside, a small girl with auburn ringlets is reading to my sleeping father.

"What are you reading, Molly?"

"*Goodnight Moon.* He likes it."

Tall, stately, and with just a touch of gray in his hair, Peter Martin is still physically my father, but his dementia is slowly robbing us of our close relationship. I pull the edge of his blanket up to his neck.

"I remember him reading that book to me." I don't mention that it must have been a favorite book because in my mind's eye I can also remember my mother reading *Goodnight Moon* to me. Even now, I can hear the rhythmic sound of her voice telling the telephone and the little old lady good night.

I watch Molly tuck the book under his exposed, pale hand. At eight, Molly is Sunshine Village's favorite guest. She is the granddaughter of Heidi Shapiro, the ringleader of the Mah jongg group. The group plays daily but the five players alternate playing in the card room, the library, or their own rooms. Molly's grandmother is the only Mah jongg player I always recognize. Heidi's hair, nails, and lipstick never vary in their matching shade of pink.

Because Molly's mother died recently after being stung by a bee in Sunshine Village's garden, Molly has visited her grandmother so much during the past few months that no one has had the heart to enforce the "No Children" rule. Most of the residents treat her like an adopted pet wandering the halls of Sunshine Village.

"Molly, why are you in here instead of at the Halloween Festival downstairs?"

Molly gives me the look only an eight-year-old can give an adult. "I told you, I was reading to him. I stopped by to visit this morning, but he had company. When I came back a little while ago, he handed me the book and kept saying 'Read, Carrie.' It was okay to read it to him, wasn't it?"

"Of course, honey. See how calm he is?"

We stand by his bed watching my father's chest barely rising and falling as he sleeps.

The door to my father's room creaks. Inching it open is the same man who covered Carolyn with a sheet. He peeks into the room. "There you are, pumpkin. Time for the pageant." He comes inside the room, then stops, becoming aware that I am here, too. I guess we both are poor observers. He didn't see me and I failed to notice Molly's in a pumpkin costume made up by her wearing green tights, an orange leotard, and carrying a brown wrist purse.

His chocolate eyes and wavy, auburn hair, the same shade as Molly's curls, are enough to let anyone know he is her dad. I was too busy looking at Carolyn earlier to recognize him as Michael Shapiro. Sunshine gossip claims he is a good catch, a young widower and an accomplished lawyer with Goram & Davis, shocked by his wife's unexpected death.

Thinking back to what the Mah jongg player yelled about Babyface, I remember that the latter gossip is attributed to Michael's successful handling of the malicious mischief case against Mrs. Schwartz. She was arrested last year for keying another resident's car because she believed he was a Nazi. Mrs. Schwartz was guilty as they come, but somehow Michael got her off scot free. Being a lawyer myself, I'm not so sure about his legal abilities. I recall hearing he works in the collections department of his firm.

"Sorry," he says, "I hope she isn't bothering either of you." He glances toward the bed.

"Not at all. We always enjoy a visit from Molly." I walk around the bed to usher them to the door. I know I'm not being polite, but I want them to leave. I don't know how long my father has been sleeping. Even though I want to ask him questions about my mother deserting us, instead, I may have to break the news to him that she is dead.

I have to make sense of why my mother came back into our lives and why just as suddenly she was killed at Sunshine Village. Is my father in danger? I may never understand my relationship with my mother or what happened between my parents, but I guess the lessons of love, healing, and redemption that my father preached from the pulpit hit their mark. No one deserves to be murdered without someone finding out who killed the person and why.

It doesn't seem to me that the police are as worried as I am that there might be a killer on the loose. I would have expected them to put the building on lockdown when they arrived, or at least when they found Carolyn, but they never did.

Until Michael and Molly leave, I don't feel comfortable opening the letter or waking my father. Michael doesn't budge, but he holds his hand out to Molly. She skips to him. I am trying so hard to remember the last time I skipped that I trip over one of my father's slippers. It disappears under the bed.

Bending down to retrieve the slipper, a fuzzy pipe cleaner under the bed catches my eye. I reach for it while looking across the floor under the bed for any other stray objects. A pair of sensible oxfords has joined Michael's dress blacks and Molly's dancing slippers. Straightening, I pocket the pipe cleaner next to the waiting envelope.

CHAPTER EIGHT

The white oxfords belong to Marta, who apparently has determined that Mrs. Schwartz doesn't need her anymore. I don't know if my bumping the bed or Marta coming in woke him, but my father's eyes are open, although he isn't saying anything. His eyes are following Marta as she reaches for his arm to take his blood pressure. It seems bizarre to me to see my active father miss all the excitement. Not that long ago, he not only would have been in the very middle of anything going on, but, despite his respected role in the community, he probably would have been any mischief's chief instigator.

As Marta rolls up the blood pressure cuff, I lean over to give my father a kiss. He pulls away from me so swiftly that the book Molly carefully placed under his hand slips from his clutch. I grab it before it reaches the floor.

"Who are you?" he asks me. I drop the book into his recliner and walk back around the bed so he can see me clearly.

"Dad, it's me. Carrie. Your daughter."

He shakes his head. "No, you're not. I have a daughter named Carrie and you're not her."

Startled, I pick up one of his pillows to fluff. I glance at Marta, who is recording his blood pressure results.

"Carrie isn't a good girl," my father adds.

I try to make light of his comment while tucking his pillow back under his head. "I hear she's a very good girl and loving daughter."

"Nope." He turns his face away from me. "She does what she wants. Hardly comes to visit."

Before I can sputter a response, Marta puts her hand on my shoulder and gives it a light squeeze. "Now, Mr. Martin," she says while looking at me, "that's not true. You probably get more visits from Carrie than most people here get from all of their children combined. You'll remember more when we get that urinary infection of yours under control. We'll all leave now so you can get some more sleep."

She snaps his bedside lamp off and probably for my benefit adds, "I'll bet once that medicine I gave you at noon kicks in, you'll be as clear-headed as you were this morning. Amazing how quickly urinary infections can affect memory and balance."

I'm very grateful to Marta. Not only does she take excellent care of my father, but Marta takes care of me, too.

Turning away from thanking her, I realize Michael and Molly are still in the room. He checks his watch. "Molly, I think we've missed the parade time."

"That's okay. I was only going so you could see the costumes."
He hugs her.

"Carrie, seems your dad has nodded off again," Michael observes. "Tell you what. Come up to my mom's place. The Maj girls went there to escape the chaos. You look like you could use a slice of pound cake."

Molly nods. Apparently, the little pumpkin isn't all that into being part of a parade but she definitely likes her grandmother's pound cake. I am about to say no, but I can't pass up the chance to interview the Mah jongg gang in Mrs. Shapiro's apartment before Brian figures out that's where they are. Besides, a slice of pound cake couldn't hurt.

CHAPTER NINE

"I tell you, we're all prisoners here. They can do anything they want to us and we don't have any say. I certainly don't feel safe here after what happened to poor Carolyn Holt. If you do, you're fools. Heidi, with all the shenanigans going on at Sunshine Village, I wouldn't be surprised if we don't find out your daughter-in-law was murdered, too. After all, she was too smart not to have her epinephrine with her. If you ask—"

"Don't be *meshnganah*." Michael's mother, Heidi, interrupts whoever is speaking. I can't pinpoint the woman whose raspy voice, as if from a lifetime of smoking, Heidi hushes. I think she probably is sitting in one of the two tufted chairs that face the brocaded couch where Hannah Schwartz and Heidi Shapiro sit. It doesn't matter. The damage has been done. We can all see it by the way Molly clings to her father.

The silence of the moment is broken when a short woman carrying a cleaver steps out of the kitchen area and approaches Molly. My muscles involuntarily tense when I see the cleaver in her hand and I try to step between Molly and the woman I recognize as the same one who followed Barbara Balfour out of the elevator. "Molly, don't pay attention to that silliness," the cleaver woman says. "Come help me get everyone a piece of cake. You can have the biggest slice."

She offers her free hand to the child. Molly doesn't smile but she lets go of her dad to obey the woman. Michael and I trail them to the table where there are two cakes. Michael says, in a loud voice, "Nobody makes a better marble cake than Mrs. Berger."

Cleaver lady, now identified as Mrs. Berger, smiles as she uses the cleaver to cut a slab of her chocolate marble cake. Not quite five feet tall, she has the most authoritative voice and demeanor I've ever encountered. It is a no-brainer to accept the generous slice of marble cake she serves me rather than ask for a smaller piece from the untouched pound cake.

Holding his fork and plate in mid-air, Michael bends to give Mrs. Berger's curly head a quick peck. He has to almost shout to be heard over the women who have resumed chattering about what transpired downstairs. "Unlike my mother, who specializes in store bought, Mrs. Berger has been baking this same cake every fifth week for almost forty years. That's . . ." he pauses for a moment while he makes a show of calculating using his fingers, ". . . four hundred or so marble cakes she has served my mother, Hannah Schwartz, Ella Goldring, and the dearly departed Sadie Moscowitz."

Mrs. Berger beams and is about to say something, but she is cut off by a voice loudly warning, "Watch your tongue, young man. Sadie was a wonderful fifth."

I almost jump because until then I hadn't noticed the wisp of a woman who was blocking Carolyn's door sitting behind me at a card table in the corner of the living room. Michael hangs his head as if chastised by her scolding. I look more closely at what she is doing at the table.

She is turning ivory Mah jongg tiles face down in an open square made by the positioning of a plastic rack in front of what would be each seat for four players. Once she finishes mixing or shuffling the tiles, she places one tile above another one, two high next to each other flush along the length of the rack. From somewhere in my memory, I recall that what she is doing is building the walls the players will pick their tiles from.

"Do you play Mah jongg? I thought a game might take our minds off the tragedy downstairs." She points at Heidi and Hannah. "They can't seem to get focused for a game today."

Looking at the pile of tissues in Mrs. Schwartz's lap and the way Heidi is trying to comfort her, I understand why neither is in the mood to play today. "Sorry, I never learned Mah jongg. I hear it is a fun game."

She shrugs and silently continues building the walls. I glance at Michael and realize from his twinkling eyes that his bowed head hid him stifling a laugh. I sidle closer to him. He whispers, "That's Mrs. Goldring. She seems flighty, but she doesn't miss a thing. Also, don't mourn for Sadie. She moved to Poughkeepsie last month to be nearer her son. When she was here, they all complained behind her back. They're delighted to be able to choose a new fifth."

"Fifth?" I'm confused as I only see four places at the table Mrs. Goldring is sitting at.

"One person is always out. You can play with four, but most groups prefer to have five players. My mom's game has been having try-outs by rotating possible fifths in and out before they make a final selection. If you want to know the truth, I think it's merely a way for the four regulars to pick up some new gossip."

I make a face at Michael. As we move closer to where his mother is seated, I ask him if there are any leading contenders for the fifth slot.

Nearing the conversation area, I see through the window behind them that Michael's mother's apartment has the same view overlooking Sunshine Village's Japanese garden and the Wahoo community Riverwalk that my father's room has. Unlike my father's third-floor room that is large enough for a sitting area or Carolyn's stark bedroom and bath, Heidi's sixth-floor apartment has a real dining and living room and a separate bedroom and kitchen.

Although I can't see who is seated on the two overstuffed chairs facing the brocaded couch, the chairs fascinate me. I haven't seen drum-style chairs with tufting like that since I was a child. The distinctive voice I heard when we first arrived coming from one of the chairs brings me back from my interior design fixation at the same time that Michael says, "Right now, Carolyn Holt and Lindy Carleton are getting the most playing time."

"Lindy Carleton?"

"You know her?"

"Indirectly," I mutter, now able to see the voice in the tufted chair belongs to Lindy Carleton. I know I must be staring, but I can't stop. This is the first time since my father has lived here that I've seen Heidi Shapiro sitting still. Her pink-painted fingertips, the exact shade of her lipstick, are pressed firmly together while platinum bee-hived Lindy Carleton talks a mile a minute. Watching them bicker would normally amuse me, but today it is taking everything I have to hold it together to gather as much information as I can before Brian figures out that all of the Mah jongg players are in Heidi's apartment. Most importantly, I have to quickly figure out a way to politely shut up Lindy Carleton, the mother of my boss.

CHAPTER TEN

When I was hired at Carleton Industries, a painting hung in the building's lobby—a formal, full-length, backlit portrait of Lindy Carleton and her late husband, James Carleton III. A few months later, the picture was replaced with a more relaxed one of James Carleton IV in hunting attire with his dog. Word at the water cooler was that Fourth had toiled in the shadow of his dead father and the scorn of his mother long enough, so when she slipped and cracked her pelvis, he shipped her off to Sunshine Village and replaced her portrait.

Except for the cane leaning against the right side of Lindy's chair in Heidi Shapiro's living room, clueing me that Lindy might be a little slow in the walking department, everything else about her appears to be intact.

I move closer to hear what she is saying, but Ella Goldring, who silently left the Mah jongg table, glues herself to me. "Heidi will never let her be our fifth," she whispers. "They're both alpha dogs, you know." She turns, making sure Michael and I are both aware of the big wink she gives us before she wanders off as quietly as she appeared.

Michael shrugs and moderates his own voice. "Mrs. Goldring's doctor attributes her diminished impulse control to her latest stroke, but my mother claims Ella has always flipped between the past and present so long as the topic is me, me, me."

I laugh, then pull myself back to my two immediate problems:

not letting myself fall apart and finding a way to interrupt Lindy's stream of negative comments about Sunshine Village.

Before I can think of a polite strategy, Molly does it for me. She plops herself onto the brocaded couch between Mrs. Schwartz and her grandmother and reaches for one of the blue-veined hands lying in Mrs. Schwartz's lap. Gently picking it up and pulling it to her, she brushes her small hand against Mrs. Schwartz's long sleeve. As her little hand pushes the sleeve up, all of us see the number tattooed on the older woman's wrist. In the moment that Lindy's attention is drawn to the indelible ink, I interject myself into Lindy's monologue.

I kneel down in front of Mrs. Schwartz with my back partially facing Lindy. "Mrs. Schwartz, I'm Carrie Martin and I was in room 346 when you left. I came upstairs with Michael to make sure you're okay."

Molly rolls her eyes while giving me one of those "Oh, please" looks. I ignore Molly because I know sometimes it takes a little white lie to get tongues wagging.

"That poor woman," Hannah Schwartz says, melting into an anguished sob. "I'm fine, but I can't understand why anyone would hurt Carolyn Holt." Her tears come harder. From the pile of tissues in her lap, I gather she hasn't been dry-eyed for long since my mother's murder. Molly glares at me. I start to say something comforting, but then my mind connects with what Mrs. Schwartz has just said. I suddenly realize everyone's belief is different than the reality of the moment.

"Mrs. Schwartz. You do realize the woman you found wasn't Ms. Holt, don't you?"

"Not Carolyn?" Heidi Shapiro says, her hands no longer still. Instead, she waves them around. From the side of my eye, I can see Lindy leaning forward in her chair.

The multiple shocks happening to me today, coupled with the analytical approach from my police training that I have tried to hold on to since Michael and I came upstairs, have allowed me to compartmentalize and downplay my emotions until now, but it is another matter to actually talk to these women about the death—no, the *murder*—of my mother. Despite scarcely knowing the woman who gave me life, I begin to lose it. It takes everything I have left to half listen to what Mrs. Schwartz says next.

"I don't understand. Carolyn and I were setting up the dining room before the children arrived for story time, when she realized she had forgotten her bag of Halloween treats. I told her to go back to her room to get the bag while I put the last few chairs out."

"Was she already wearing her Burberry outfit?"

"Of course she already had her costume on. The children were due in a few minutes. When the first children and their parents started coming in and she still wasn't back, I went to her room to see what was delaying her. Her door was open." For a second, her lips continue to move, but no words come out. Molly tightens her grip on Mrs. Schwartz's hand.

Heidi looks at the two of them. "And?" she asks.

"I walked in. She was lying on the floor with the knife sticking out of her back." Mrs. Schwartz pulls her hand out of Molly's and covers her eyes.

Lindy Carleton grabs her cane and stands. Stepping around me, she almost gets into Mrs. Schwartz's face. "Hannah," she demands, having again found her tongue. "What did you do then?"

I move back to get out of their way, but I keep my eyes focused on Mrs. Schwartz instead of giving in to my instinct to look at Lindy. Mrs. Schwartz takes her hands from her eyes and sits upright. Almost spitting in Lindy's face, she replies. "I screamed. I screamed for all I was worth. I was still screaming when Marta and Barbara Balfour ran into the room." She pauses, and then corrects herself. "No, come to think of it, only Marta came all the way in. She told Barbara to call the police."

Mrs. Schwartz stares at me as if seeing me for the first time. "You found us there," she says. "You made us leave the room." The tone of her voice is accusing. I realize Marta must have brought Mrs. Schwartz upstairs before anyone knew the body was my mother's or that Carolyn had been attacked and put in the third-floor linen closet.

"Mrs. Schwartz," I say gently. "I understand how you feel." I don't share why I am so familiar with the sensation I once again have in the pit of my stomach. I understand Mrs. Schwartz believed telling Carolyn to go back to her room caused her death. For years, I have had a similar feeling—that if I had done something, anything, differently, my mother wouldn't have left. "You didn't kill Carolyn Holt. She got banged up and put into the linen closet, but she's very much alive."

"Then who was knifed?" Heidi Shapiro asks.

"My mother," I whisper.

It doesn't matter how soft-spoken I am; Brian's voice drowns out my whisper. "The victim was Charlotte Martin, Peter Martin's ex-wife. And Carrie's mother." At his words, all turn to where he stands with Barbara Balfour near the cake table.

Although Brian is watching everyone's reactions, I can tell from his widened stance and tight jawline that he is not pleased to see me in the middle of everything. Because he has found his way to Heidi's apartment, I assume the building still is not under any kind of formal lock-down. I try to figure out a way to make myself scarce, but Brian positioned himself between the door and me.

Chapter Eleven

Stuck! Consequently, without a way out I opt to introduce Brian to Heidi, who introduces him to everyone else. As Brian works the room, including tossing a few perfunctory questions at me, I wait for a moment to escape his scrutiny. Eventually, when he takes Mrs. Schwartz aside, I flee to my father's room to see if he is awake. He isn't.

I decide to go back to my office and finish work I neglected when I had to make drafting and filing today's brief a priority. I prefer to wrap myself in work rather than think about how the day unfolded.

As I slip behind the wheel of my Honda, the envelope in my pocket bends. I pull it from my pocket, and the pipe cleaner comes out, too. I stare at the two objects in my hand puzzled by my mother taking twenty-six years to come back into my life and then leaving permanently, just a few hours later. Hoping the answer is in the unaddressed envelope, I take a deep breath. Even though I would rather have talked to my father before opening it, I can't wait any longer.

Slowly, I unfold the tightly creased letter. "My dearest daughter," it begins. "Parents . . ." That's all I can read before I am overcome with tears. I cry for my mother and for myself—that I never felt like a "dearest daughter." I cry until I tell myself it is ridiculous to cry this much for someone who walked out on me, and that if I am going to cry for anyone I should be crying for my father, who is leaving me unwillingly. Picking up the now tearstained letter, I re-read the opening words and again I can't hold back the tears.

Although I know reading it might explain much of what happened in the past, I simply can't handle it right now. I am too afraid to know. So, I thrust the envelope and the pipe cleaner—the two things that tie my mother to me—into the glove compartment. My relationship with my mother has been on hold this long; it can wait a little longer.

I drive from the Sunshine Village parking lot oblivious to the repeated jarring caused by ignoring the "sleeping policemen" cement speed bumps. I debate going home or back to the office and decide that at least at the office there is mindless work.

The ride from Sunshine Village to Carleton Industries that runs parallel to the Riverwalk is quite short. I am relieved to feel a familiar kind of comfort when I pull into the Carleton lot. Even though it is almost dusk, there are plenty of cars still here and the glass walls of the building are dotted with lights. Each light meant another employee is making money for CI, our large diversified corporate employer.

The first James Carleton invented a metal flange that better enabled the movement of guns affixed to stationary objects such as tanks or walls. James Carleton, Jr., added to the company's product line, but it was the third James Carleton who not only increased the firm's sub-tax holding company structure, but also took CI international. He understood that because flange profits are highest during wartime, having a global reach could guarantee consistent profits by tapping into the conflict of the week. Carleton IV, or Fourth, as we employees commonly call him, is the man I now work for. He is charged with preserving the company's assets, but most of the employees, including me, think he lacks the vision or inclination of his forefathers. I'm not sure whether he will sell out or leave the company intact for his only daughter, Jaimie.

I owe my job to Lindy Carleton's husband, James III's, vision. Under him, the company brought most of its legal work in-house. The CI staff now internally handles almost all of its real estate, labor-management, tax, and general corporate issues. I was hired to work on international tax projects, but so far, other than filling out expatriate tax returns, my international contact had been by phone or e-mail—frustrating for a single female whose passport has plenty of empty pages.

Until today, I've told myself that staying in Wahoo is my gift to my father. In the two years I've been with the company, friends have found new positions and encouraged me to job hunt, but I always felt my father needed me close. His not knowing me today is prompting troublesome thoughts about whether my being here comforts him or me. I know this is how dementia progresses, but actually experiencing versus intellectually understanding my father's decline is heartbreaking.

I shake my head, hoping it will clear, but it doesn't. I can't think too far into the future now. There are too many thoughts—my father's condition, who killed my mother, if Carolyn will be okay, who will bury my mother—vying for my attention.

In this disturbed frame of mind, I push through the glass doors to the lobby and stop short. Directly in front of me, his portrait over his shoulder, is James Carleton IV. I'm taken aback. Peons like me religiously work on Saturdays and Sundays, but Fourth normally spends his weekends at the yacht club. Seeing him here today, in docksiders, jeans, and a collared shirt, jars me back to reality. For a minute I think of backing out the door again, but then I realize he has seen me.

"Hello, Mr. Carleton," I blurt out. "I just saw your mother." I sound like an idiot. The look he shoots in my direction confirms, at least to me, that he probably has similar thoughts.

I have to get myself in check. Mature attorneys desirous of

promotions don't blubber in front of their boss.

"My mother?" he asks in a deep baritone voice. I nod.

Although he stands erect as he makes me feel he is evaluating me with his eyes, he has to look up at me. I decide, as I begin again, that the dog in his portrait must have been a miniature.

"I'm Carrie Martin, sir. An attorney in your legal department. I was visiting my father at Sunshine Village and happened to see your mother in Mrs. Shapiro's apartment." Maybe it is what has happened today or the tension of being face to face with my boss, but I can't stop talking like a train about to wreck. "Your mom is getting around so much better than right after her accident."

"That she is," he concedes. I can tell from the relaxation of his face muscles and posture that Fourth has made the connection between my father and me. He confirms this by asking, "Your father is Peter Martin, the minister of the church on Oakwood?"

"He *was* the minister there. He moved into Sunshine Village almost three years ago."

"A good man." For a moment his face softens, much like the portrait in which he is patting his dog, so I know he now remembers why my father left his pulpit. "How long have you been working for us, now?"

"A little over two years, sir."

"In what area?"

"International tax."

I shift my weight from foot to foot as he continues to look at me. I don't have any idea what he is thinking but as uncomfortable as I am with his scrutiny, I force myself to not say anything. Finally, he continues. "Martin, be at my office at eight tomorrow. I have an assignment I think you would be perfect for." Giving me no chance to reply or question him, he walks away. I stand in shock watching his back before reversing my direction and retracing my steps out of the building. Work can wait. I need to put my feet up with a glass of wine to sort out today. No, make that a bottle of wine.

Chapter Twelve

The alarm buzzing at 5:45 on Monday morning hurts my ears. I didn't finish off the entire bottle last night, but I made a pretty good dent in it—something I've been doing a little too often since my life fell into the pattern of work, gym, and Dad. I usually love to hit the snooze button, but today I want to be standing in Fourth's outer office before eight. I don't know what he has in mind for me to do, but I certainly don't want to appear hungover or be late for whatever it is.

Not a problem. I'm actually in the hall twenty minutes early—ten minutes before Fourth's secretary arrives to unlock the door to his office suite. He walks in at exactly eight and motions me to follow him into his inner office. I fall into step behind him. Although Fourth is taking full strides, I have to be careful not to step on his heels.

"Martin, I assume I can trust your discretion."

"Yes, sir." I have no idea what I'm promising to be discreet about.

He points me to the guest chair across from his massive cherry-mahogany desk. While he settles himself behind his desk, I note that it is a far cry from my gunmetal gray relic downstairs.

Today I am more in control of myself. Instead of filling the silence, I wait for him to explain what task he has in mind for me.

"We're in the midst of a privately brought lawsuit. It isn't important for you to know the details—only that we are cooperating fully." He pulls a yellow legal pad closer to him. "We turned over the documents originally requested so they would see there was nothing to pursue, but they weren't happy. They filed a Motion to Produce that the judge granted over our objection. Today, their attorney will be going through our project-related cabinets marking documents they want to copy."

"But," I interrupt, "aren't all our files electronic?"

Fourth tightens his grip on the pad while furrowing his brows. "They are asking for documents that predate when we went digital. Tomorrow morning, we'll have an opportunity to object to any of the documents they mark today. We've agreed to deliver final copies on Wednesday."

Motions and rulings. It sounds as if the lawsuit or investigation already has proceeded pretty far. If it were about a tax or regulatory issue, I think I would be aware of it. That means whatever the case involves probably concerns one of the areas I don't work in.

As Fourth continues ranting about this being a wild goose chase, I wonder why he is personally involved in a discovery matter. Most document discovery is so routine that any member of the in-house CI legal team can handle it. I rack my brain trying to remember any news story that might have resulted in Carleton Industries being involved in litigation or that Fourth might have a special interest in.

The only thing I can think of is a story a local television news reporter did last year. His TV footage showed a few dead fish in the Wahoozee River that he alleged had been killed by waste products being released from CI's manufacturing site near the Riverwalk. If I remember right, he made a big deal of how, once again, the Wahoo affiliate is always on the public's side because the complainant had called the EPA, OSHA, Wahoo News, and TV station, but no one except him followed up on the story.

Once the TV reporter's story ran, everyone else jumped to

get in on the action. CI acted stunned, apologized, paid a fine, and continued manufacturing. No new dead fish have been reported lately so the story fell out of the news. Unless today's discovery has something to do with something that has been kept out of the news, I bet that's what the lawsuit is about.

"I want you, as one of our company's lawyers, to walk around behind their lawyer today." Fourth comes around his desk with the legal pad. "When their representative numbers a drawer or stickers a document, I don't want you to get in the way, but write down whatever he marks for copying." He taps the top of the pad with his index finger. "Make sure you mark the top of each page of this pad 'attorney-client privilege.' And don't forget," he says, handing me the pad, "I'll need the drawer number and the specific document stickered."

Fourth perches on the corner of his desk. When I nod that I understand my task, he adds, "Don't discuss anything besides the weather with their person. At the end of the day, bring your list back to me. Only me—not even my secretary. Understand?" I nod again. "Good. You can wait in my outside office until they get here," he says, dismissing me with a flick of his hand.

For a moment I stay seated, but as he moves around his desk, I hurry toward his door wondering what he plans to do with my confidential work product. It isn't unusual to have a lowly staff member like me involved in shadowing discovery production, but why all the secrecy? I rein in my imagination before I come up with too many unethical possibilities.

At nine on the dot, the opposition arrives—two people. The first is a lawyer who leaves once he finds out Carleton Industries is granting access without a screaming hissy fit. The one who stays behind to do the nerd work is Michael Shapiro. I'm surprised to see him. "They needed someone to catalog everything. Goram & Davis is handling this case pro bono," he mumbles. I make a noncommittal response while leading him to the basement storage room. His comment pretty much confirms my belief that this case involves the dead fish, because pro bono environmental work is something Goram & Davis often takes on.

"Awkward" definitely is the word of the moment. Michael apparently doesn't head the collections department. He appears to merely be a briefcase carrier for the big boys. Today, he acts like a kid caught with his hand in the cookie jar while I uncomfortably follow Fourth's directions of not fraternizing with the enemy.

From nine to four, with a short break for lunch, during which we go our separate ways, he opens drawers and reads each document. Each time he pushes his reading glasses back on his nose and bends to mark a document with a sticker, I dutifully notate my list. There is no small talk between us. At four, after walking him back to our lobby, I take the elevator to Mr. Carleton's office.

The outside suite is deserted, but I hear voices coming from the Fourth's inner office. I knock and wait. Instead of yelling, "Come in," Fourth opens the door and ushers me in. Another man is in the office, standing, with his back to me, on the far side of the office. Because of where Fourth had me sit this morning, I never really took in the significance of the wall the man is staring at. It actually is a huge window that overlooks the building's interior atrium.

I eat lunch in the atrium every day and often look up at the frescoed wall one sees from there. Who knew that, all this time, I've been staring at a one-way mirror? How sneaky—or creepy—can Fourth—or one of his predecessors—get? I wonder, if the family went to the expense of putting in a disguised one-way mirror, if they bug the atrium for sound, too. Because I am so fixated on the windowed wall, I don't notice Fourth holding his hand out for my list until he clears his throat.

"Ms. Martin." Mr. Carleton's voice snaps me back to attention. "This is Lester Balfour, vice-president of . . ."

I don't catch his complete title as I'm trying to figure out if this distinguished, gray-templed man telling me how sorry he is about my mother's recent death is related to Barbara. He seems to be too old to be her husband. It is only when I notice that Lester has the same steel-blue eyes as she does that I realize he probably is her father. Now I know how, without donating a wing or making a big monetary contribution, Fourth was able to jump his mother to the top of Sunshine Village's wait list when she needed assisted living after she broke her pelvis.

Without looking at it, Fourth hands my legal pad to Lester, who flips through its pages. Both Fourth and I wait silently for Mr. Balfour to say something. I'm uncertain what he is looking for or how they plan to use my notes; but, based upon the butterflies in my stomach, I don't have a good feeling about any of this.

Mr. Balfour interrupts me, convincing myself lawyers and businessmen often exhibit a bit of paranoia. "B2-2 refers to?"

"Basement—filing cabinet 2—document 2. I put the abbreviation key on the last page. The cabinets in each room are stickered."

Balfour examines the pages again. If I wasn't watching him intently, I might have missed the nod he gives Fourth.

Just that quickly Fourth once again dismisses me. I think about going to my office to catch up on the real work I should have been doing for the past two days or to pick up the two contracts sitting on my desk so I can read them at home tonight, but I decide office work can wait. First comes my need to get some answers from my father.

CHAPTER THIRTEEN

My heart skips a beat when I see my father's bed is empty. Scared, I look around the room and am relieved to see Marta putting a handful of linens on the window ledge. "My father?"

"Oh, honey," Marta says, "nothing to get upset about. Your dad is visiting Ms. Holt. She's back, you know?" She strips my father's sheets and throws them onto his recliner. I am confused as to why Marta, instead of one of the aides, is changing my father's sheets.

"When did you start changing linens?"

Marta chuckles. "We're a little short-handed so I'm helping out. How are you doing, Carrie?"

"I'm okay." Between the police questioning me, giving my official statement, and trying to juggle work, my father, and making funeral arrangements for when the police release my mother's body, I'm feeling harried, but to Marta I simply repeat, "I'm okay."

She picks up a pillow and pulls its case off so roughly, the case catches and rips. "Darn pillowcase." Grabbing a clean pillowcase from the pile, she turns her face away from me.

"Marta, what's wrong?"

She shakes her head, but I press her until she admits, "I thought I better find a way to keep myself busy while everyone is stopping by Ms. Holt's room to welcome her back. I don't want to run into Mrs. Carleton." I wrinkle my face in confusion. "Mrs. Carleton told Ms. Balfour she doesn't want me coming into her room anymore. She wants me 'fired for my slovenly ways.' " Marta stands straight, leaving the pillow sitting on the bed. "I may not be the brightest bulb, but I'm not a pig!"

"Far from it," I assure her. "Surely Ms. Balfour knows you're everyone's favorite nurse."

"I don't know about that." Marta gives a modest little smile. "I aim to please. In the six years I've been here, I've seen a lot of people simply putting in their shifts. They'd just as soon take a smoke break as help a patient get to the garden or dining room. And," she adds, lowering her voice, "I've seen a lot of folks at all levels with sticky fingers."

She clamps her lips closed and finishes putting on the clean pillowcase. Watching her carefully position a new pad over my father's bottom sheet, I can't imagine anyone having anything but good thoughts about Marta. "What does Lindy have against you?"

"I wouldn't hang her pants."

"Excuse me?" Marta refusing to do anything for a resident doesn't sound right to me. "Her slacks?"

"Yes, her slacks. Mrs. Carleton's son pays for her to have general assistance. You know, an aide or nurse comes in to check on her at scheduled times unless there is an emergency." I nod. I am fully aware of the levels of care and payment schedule because I have been trying to ascertain how I will pay for more advanced care for my father.

"Whichever one of us is scheduled to round Mrs. Carlton always asks if there is anything we can do for her, but she rarely needs anything when we poke our heads in. Instead, she waits for us to leave and then calls the front desk for someone to come upstairs right away to help her."

"And?" I prompt her to continue explaining why she is so upset.

Marta expertly tucks the edges of the sheets under the mattress to make perfect hospital corners. "Usually her 'emergency' is wanting us to pick up a Kleenex from the floor or to hang her slacks because she can't manage the clips on the hangers with her arthritis. I've always been glad to hang her pants or do whatever else she needs when I'm not busy."

"Couldn't she just use the paper roller hangers that come from the dry cleaners?"

"Not Mrs. Carleton. She hates them. Whether she's already worn a pair of pants or they've just been delivered from the cleaners, they have to be switched to a clip hanger so they don't get a roller crease." I check my own slacks. Other than wrinkles from my sitting in them, they don't show any marks.

"A few weeks ago, Mrs. Carleton called the desk and they radioed me. I told them to tell her I'd be there as soon as I finished settling my patient into his wheelchair. I guess I wasn't speedy enough."

"I don't see how taking a few extra minutes to get to her room would put you in the doghouse."

"Well, she complained about me to Ms. Balfour. Ms. Balfour listened to my version of the incident and while she seemed to agree with me, she told me we had to make nice to Mrs. Carleton. She basically ordered me to accompany her to Mrs. Carleton's room to apologize. Ms. Balfour did explain to Mrs. Carleton that there is a higher level of assistance she can pay for. Mrs. Carleton denied needing a higher level of help. She then went into a tirade. Said for what they pay, the residents are little more than prisoners with bad food and barely passable service."

"I'm sure that went over well."

Marta rolls her eyes as she lays a blanket on the bed. "Ms. Balfour told Mrs. Carleton, 'Sunshine Village takes no prisoners, so feel free to make other arrangements.' When Mrs. Carleton reminded her that anyone who wants to leave has to give thirty days notice, Ms. Balfour didn't miss a beat. She personally waived the notice requirement. We started to leave. Ms. Balfour was right behind me when Ms. Carleton called, 'Barbara, would you please hang up the pants on the couch.' "

Marta and I both laugh at the image of Barbara having to clip Lindy's pants as Marta retrieves the pillows from the windowsill and puts them on the bed. "But if that was a few weeks ago, what is Lindy still doing here?" I ask.

"Being ornery, bless her heart."

"It sounds like you only have to lay low a few more days until she moves."

"That's why I'm in here doing your father's sheets instead of in Room 346."

"Room 346?" I'm shocked. How could they put Carolyn back in the room where my mother was killed? I've tried to leave the investigation in Brian's capable hands, but thoughts of why my mother is dead and whodunit intrude into even my dreams. At times, I've wondered if Carolyn may have been the intended victim? Now, hearing that Carolyn is back in the room my mother died in, I feel a chill and know I have goosebumps. "I would think Barbara Balfour would have moved her."

"She was going to, but Ms. Holt wouldn't hear of it."

"But my mother was murdered in Room 346," I protest.

"Carrie, I can't fathom wanting to move back into a room where someone close to those you love was murdered, but once the police released the room, it was cleaned for occupancy immediately. Even if hadn't been ready when she came back, Ms. Holt would have waited for her old room. She isn't going anywhere else." She gives me a quizzical look. "You and your father are probably the only two people who don't realize Carolyn Holt is sweet on your dad."

"What?"

"Ms. Holt likes being near your father so much that when

you moved him to his new room, she chose to downsize from her suite of rooms to 346, the only room available on this floor."

I so associate Carolyn with Room 346 that I forgot she used to have a full-sized, independent-living apartment like Heidi Shapiro's. Subconsciously, I guess I assumed she downsized to save money. Marta's explanation reminds me why I should never "assume" things. Because Carolyn is so involved in planning and participating in everything going on at Sunshine Village, I didn't think about her paying extra fees for assistance she never uses.

Looking out my father's window, I take in the beauty of the Japanese-style garden. A wealthy benefactor supposedly donated it to get his mother to the top of the wait list. From my father's room, I can see the entire garden and the beautifully landscaped entrance Sunshine Village residents use to access the River-walk's benches and lookout points. The entrance also is fairly close to one of the manmade sets of stairs that lead from the Riverwalk to the Wahoozee River. The Japanese garden and the back of the main Sunshine Village building, in which most of the apartments are located, run parallel to the Riverwalk and the water. My view of the retirement home's rarely used second entrance leading to the undeveloped part of the Riverwalk is blocked by a stand of trees adjacent to the formal Japanese garden.

Carolyn's former rooms also faced the garden. Maybe Marta is right. Something motivated my friend to give up both space and view. Needing assisted living is one thing, but even I, who prefers to avoid nature, wouldn't willingly trade a garden view and independent living for a room facing the street and parking lot unless I had an ulterior motive—like a crush on someone.

"I can see why my father spends so much time looking out his window. The rocks, the red bridge, the flowers, unique trees, and special plants really do make one forget the reality of this building."

Marta scoops up the used linens she threw onto the recliner and comes to stand next to me by the window. "It is beautiful," she acknowledges. "I hope we're able to keep it looking this good. Our groundskeepers only mow and spray for weeds."

I peer more closely at the garden. It has had more than mowing and weed-kill care.

"When Jess Shapiro was alive, she volunteered two afternoons a week helping Sunshine's garden club tend the Japanese garden. Without her guidance, I don't know if there are any gardening club members who can keep things as beautiful as they are now. I doubt Barbara Balfour will pay anyone to do the work Jess did."

As I listen to Marta, I don't care about the garden as much as I do about little Molly. Michael seems to have an interest in her and Heidi and her friends definitely are well intentioned, but I feel for the child. I know what it's like growing up without a mother. The ladies in the congregation all stood in as mother figures for me, but it wasn't the same. Even Carolyn, who probably stepped up the most, couldn't replace my mother.

My father tried to be both parents, and I love him for that, but still, until yesterday, it wasn't enough. Now, of course, knowing my mother had thoughts of killing him and rejected taking me with her when she left, my feelings are all conflicted.

CHAPTER FOURTEEN

"Hello, Carrie," my father says as I walk into Carolyn's room. Someone has pulled Carolyn's recliner near her bed for him to sit in. Barbara Balfour sits next to him on a rolling chair she must have snitched from the nurse's station, while Detective Brian is perched on the window ledge behind Barbara and Dad. Carolyn, in a pink, flowered bed jacket, is propped up in bed listening to Molly read her a book, and Heidi, Lindy, and someone I don't know are rearranging the top of Carolyn's dresser where plants and balloons people sent are competing for space.

Except for me, no one seems to care or even remember that this is the room my mother was murdered in. In fact, the atmosphere is so like a three-ring circus that I assume the "party" has been going on for quite a while.

Carolyn's head is less swollen than I expected, but gravity has caused the blood to run downward, making the left side of her face pretty gruesome. The darkness of the bruising tells me she is a long way from the yellow and green fade-away stage. With a wave of her hand, she acknowledges my presence, but doesn't disturb Molly's reading by speaking.

I give my father a hug and kiss, holding him a moment longer than usual because I am so relieved he knows me. Frightening how much his acknowledgement validates me—especially because at some time in the future he won't come back to me. With one arm still slung around my father's thin shoulder, I smile at Barbara and Brian as I try to determine if the two of them are focusing on my father rather than Carolyn.

The resemblance between Barbara and her father is obvious. Something about both Balfours rubs me the wrong way, though, until now, I've not given much thought to what it is I don't like. Perhaps it is the way each can appear engaged while already having dismissed one from any ongoing dialogue. "It" is probably what makes her such an effective executive director.

She is young for her job. Mid-thirties. Most folks would never realize she wears a uniform, but she is always fully made-up, has on a skirt that shows her legs off to maximum advantage, and sports heels that add three to four inches to her height. I'm actually jealous of her below-shoulder-length, brown hair. Unlike mine, it has the bounce and sheen of a television-commercial model.

Keeping a smile pasted on my face, I let go of my father's shoulder and sit myself firmly on the wide armrest of the faux-leather recliner. "I'm glad things have calmed down a bit."

"Excuse me?" Barbara says.

"The two of you and my father look like you've been having such a nice long visit, I assumed things have slowed down for you." I ignore the three women fussing over the flowers and deliberately avoid making eye contact with Brian because I can almost predict the expression that will be plastered on his face. Barbara begins to say something, but I quickly continue. "Maybe I shouldn't assume. You know what they say about that word."

She laughs. "No, things still are hectic, but I'm a believer in making time for our residents." She reaches over and pats my father's hand. Her smile matches mine. "Detective McPhillips and I came to see Ms. Holt, but most of Sunshine Village had the same idea, so we've been visiting with your father instead." She pats his hand again. I wish my father would swat her like he would a summer gnat.

"More people should have your attitude," I say. The armrest is feeling uncomfortable so I stand. "Carolyn always stresses how important visits are."

"That's exactly what we were talking about. Your dad was telling us about Charlotte coming to visit."

Barbara stands and straightens the pleats of her skirt as she lets me digest what she said. I don't respond. She starts to leave, but my curiosity gets the best of me. "He *knows* she came to visit?" I work at keeping my voice low and innocent. "When I was here yesterday, he didn't know anyone. Marta said he had a urinary infection, but that once the antibiotics took effect he'd be himself again. Happily," I add, "he seems to be."

"Oh, he is," Brian assures me from the window ledge.

"But yesterday?"

"Yesterday, Carrie, I was fine." My father looks at me warily. From the way he touches his forehead, I recognize he's afraid he has forgotten something. Recently, he told me the hardest part of his disease is actually knowing he is forgetting or that he is repeating himself, but not being able to do anything about it. "Believe me, I didn't hallucinate Charlotte visiting me."

"I know you didn't, Dad." After all, I have concrete evidence—the piece of pipe cleaner I found under his bed.

Barbara steps closer to me. Her heels make her level with me in my flats. "Apparently, from what your father tells us, Charlotte visited him before she went to see Ms. Holt."

"We're still trying to figure out the time sequence from when your mother left your office, Carrie, to when she was found," Brian explains. "It appears that she made multiple visits to Sunshine Village, but Ms. Holt doesn't remember much between the time she was hit and coming to in the closet in her boots. Her doctor isn't sure she'll ever get those moments back."

"I hope she does," Barbara interrupts. She moves closer to

Brian, keeping her eyes trained on him. "I can't begin to tell you how grateful Sunshine Village is for the way the Wahoo police are handling this case, but we simply can't wait for this to become past history. It's too distressing a situation for our residents."

Brian blushes at Barbara's compliments. While he acts like a sap, I challenge Barbara. "I wouldn't have thought to classify my mother's death as a distressing situation."

"Nor do we," she quickly assures me, with a shake of her hair. She holds up a finger to let Marta, who is waving at her from the hallway, know she will be with her in a moment. Barbara turns back to me and continues, "Sadly, we have to deal with people's passing all the time. Over the years, we've learned to distract our residents while we quickly clean the room. Our goal always is to minimize upsetting everyone longer than necessary. Unfortunately, discussions and media coverage have kept this situation in the limelight."

I have no response, nor would it matter because Barbara is already in the hall with Marta. Now I know what makes Barbara so good at her job. In addition to her looks, confidence, and ability to think on her feet, she has absolutely no integrity.

CHAPTER FIFTEEN

I take the chair Barbara was sitting in. It rolls under my weight. Although she is shorter than I am, I can't imagine Barbara is that much lighter, but the chair didn't shift under her. Chalk another one up for Ms. Perfect. I know I'm acting catty and I can't imagine why until Brian clears his throat.

"Red," he says softly. I ignore him and concentrate on my father.

"Dad," I say, resting my fingers on his hand—the mirror image of mine. "I need you to answer a few questions for me." He doesn't answer, but he is paying attention.

"My mo—Charlotte came to see me yesterday," I begin.

"She came to see me, too."

"Yes, I know. What did she want?" My detective side is taking over. I wonder if she was opening or closing her bag when the pipe cleaner broke and fell under his bed. I'm also curious what she was getting out or putting into the bag.

"She told me she was ready to see you, but didn't know where to find you. I told her you were at your office."

This time, I look at Brian. Now, we know for sure how my mother knew I'd be at CI on a Sunday. I also understand Brian and Barbara's earlier comments about my mother's multiple visits to Sunshine Village. Because my father told her where to find me, but she wasn't found dead until after she visited CI, she had to have been at Sunshine Village at least twice.

"What did she want to tell me, Dad?"

He looks at me, perplexed. "You know. She came back after seeing you and told me she had shared everything with you and left you the envelope." My father moves his hand away from mine as he becomes agitated. "Didn't she give you the envelope?"

"Oh, she did." I soothe him. "But I thought once she talked to me, she wouldn't need to see you again."

He turns in his chair to make eye contact with me. "That's exactly why she came back. She wanted to tell me that she had done it. She wanted me to know everything finally is as it should be." My father observes me carefully. When I was a child, he could look through me as if he had a truth-meter.

"She gave it to me and we talked, but under the circumstances I thought I should make sure what she told me is the truth. That she left you because she was afraid she would hurt you."

"Charlotte could never have done that." His eyes drift to the window, even though this room doesn't have a decent view, and I know I am losing him.

To keep him in the present, I hasten to add, "She said she loved you too much to take a chance of hurting you."

"Or you." He begins to rock back and forth.

I quickly ask, "But why did she come back to Wahoo now?"

"Yes, why?" Brian asks. I jump. I forgot he was there, listening.

For a moment, I selfishly hope while Brian is in the room, my father does fade away. "Brian, what's going on?" Although I keep myself aligned to watch Brian's body language, from the corner of my eye, I see Carolyn shift herself in her bed. I'm not certain if she still is paying Molly's reading any attention or is completely focused on listening to my conversation with Brian.

I nag at him again. "Brian, are you trying to conduct some type of interview with all these people here? What exactly are you trying to find out?"

Brian leans back against the window. He appears tired, and I can sense his frustration—either from running into dead ends or from trying to decide whether to handle me tenderly for having lost my mother or aggressively for not telling him about the envelope containing her letter and then for getting in his face. My father continues to face the window, or perhaps he is staring at Brian.

"I'm sorry," Brian says. "This has been a tough day and I'm not trying to make it more difficult for you, but questions keep coming up that I have to find answers for. You know how it is."

And I do. I relax as I get up and say, "Join the I-wish-I-knew-the-answer club."

Brian's neck reddens ever so slightly. When his neck does that, I know I have pushed him to a point of anger or embarrassment. Neither is what I want to do to the detective handling my mother's murder. "Brian, I'm sorry, too. This whole thing has me on edge. I've been trying to hold it together since my mother . . ." And then I lose it. I can't hold the tears back.

Brian springs from the ledge and puts his arms around me. I swallow while willing myself to stop, but whether it is his feel and smell, what's happened to my mother, or what is happening to my father, I can't regain control. Brian waits, gently stroking my hair. Even though I know all eyes in the room must be on us, I snuggle to him. For a moment I think Brian is going to kiss me in front of everyone, but then I feel my father gently touch my hand, too. My tears and the moment's mood abruptly end when Brian, whispering in my ear, asks me what was in the envelope. I pull away from him. I have forgotten how kind but cunning he can be.

Before I'm able to respond, Carolyn, who has been quietly taking in the whole scene, interrupts. "What about the envelope?" Apparently she hasn't lost her librarian's ability to listen to conversations in all parts of a room.

"My envelope," my father quietly intones while I answer Carolyn's question with everyone's eyes now glued on me.

"I don't really know," I say.

"What, you didn't open it?" Carolyn frowns at me. "I would have opened it immediately." Carolyn is the only person in the world other than my father whom I've never been able to hide the truth from. "Well?" she demands.

"I opened it," I admit. "But I got only as far as unfolding the letter and reading the words 'To My Dearest Daughter' before I couldn't stop crying." I wipe a fresh tear from my cheek and reach for the box of tissues on her nightstand. Getting myself back in control, I attempt to smile at her, and then I look sheepishly from Carolyn to Brian. "I decided to follow Scarlett O'Hara's advice and think about it tomorrow. For today, I stuck the envelope and letter back into my glove compartment."

Chapter Sixteen

Marta interrupts from the hall, shooing everyone out of Carolyn's room so she can get some privacy and rest. Brian and I fall into step walking my father back to his room. As we pass Lindy, Heidi, and Molly waiting for the elevator, Molly pipes up, "Nana wants to talk to you." She grabs my hand, hitting my side with yet another one of the little purses she is never without. I'm beginning to wonder if this kid has hand and purse fetishes.

"I'll go with your dad," Brian offers, quickly moving to catch up to my father who doesn't break his purposeful stride. As I follow Molly, I wish I had the ability my father has, when he wants it, to walk by people giving them a smile or even a touch on the shoulder by way of acknowledgement without ever stopping to become fully engaged by them.

Molly still holds my hand as she expectantly waits for her grandmother to speak. "Carrie," Heidi begins. "We're all so sorry about your mother." She gives Lindy a meaningful look.

Lindy shakes her head affirmatively and adds, "Very sorry."

"Molly and I were talking," Heidi says, "and we decided we'd like to invite you to dinner in my apartment Friday." I must appear uncomfortable about accepting an invitation to eat in one of the private apartments, having always eaten in the main dining room when visiting at Sunshine Village, because she hastens to let me know it's only a small Shabbat dinner for family and friends.

The idea of going to a dinner that has religious overtones

and customs I'm unfamiliar with makes me even more uncomfortable, so I start to give my automatic "No, thank you" when Molly pleads, "Please come. Please say yes."

I look at her and can't say anything except, "I'd be delighted. What can I bring?"

Molly squeals so loudly, I barely hear Heidi respond, "Only yourself."

Lindy Carleton clears her throat. "How lovely. You know, Heidi, I don't think I've ever been to your apartment for a Shabbat dinner."

For a moment, I imagine Heidi saying, "And you won't be coming this time either." Instead, she extends an invitation to Lindy, who immediately accepts. I guess Heidi has come to the conclusion that friends and family are welcome guests and that there are times it is best to keep your friend-enemies close.

The elevator door opens and Lindy, leaning on her cane for balance, is the first on. "Hurry," she says, pushing a button with the top of her cane while using her left hand to both steady herself and hold the door for them, "I want to take my walk before it gets dark."

Molly follows, but Heidi lingers a moment. "I'm glad you're coming. I know Michael will be pleased, too." She gets on the elevator, the doors close, and all I can think of is that I should have followed my first instinct and said "no." After the discovery debacle, I don't relish spending an evening with Michael Shapiro.

CHAPTER SEVENTEEN

"Red," Brian says, returning, "I helped your dad get settled. He's already asleep."

I am disappointed to have had so little time with my father tonight, but relieved that I can get away from Sunshine Village earlier than I anticipated.

"I bet you haven't eaten yet. Let me buy you a FattBurger."

I start to refuse because I have too much work to do. I've already lost a day with the discovery matter and will probably lose the better part of another finalizing the details and attending my mother's funeral. Brian waves off any objection. "You protest too much, Carrie. You still have to eat, and besides, this isn't really for old times' sake. I need to see the envelope and letter your mother gave you, so I thought it might be a little more palatable for you if we grab a FattBurger, too."

I laugh. Leave it to Brian to basically demand I turn over my mother's envelope while sweetening the moment by offering me my favorite junk food.

The FattBurger is a dive started in an abandoned gas station about fifteen years ago. We'd all hang out there after school or the Friday night football games, clogging our arteries with malt-eds, burgers, and fries. Delicious and greasy when I was in high school, nothing about it has changed for me since it opened. Well, maybe one thing. Instead of getting a burger almost too big to get my jaws around for $1.65, it now costs me $4.99 for that same pleasure. "Okay, you win, but I need to get a few files from my office."

"No problem. Let's go." He catches me glancing toward my father's room. Firmly taking my arm, he assures me, "He's out for the count."

We leave the building, and Brian surprises me by not turning right toward the parking lot and my car, which contains the letter I know he can't wait to open. Instead, he walks toward the Riverwalk. When I don't immediately follow him, he waits for me.

"Red," he says, looking back toward the parking lot, "your car will still be there when we get back. This sunset won't." Brian is right. The early November sun setting over the river is breathtaking. "Truce? No police talk. Just two old friends enjoying the view and catching up over a quick bite of dinner."

I certainly don't object, as long as we stop by my office first. "Not a problem," he repeats. He points to where the CI building backs up to the Riverwalk. In the distance, it is the only structure marring an otherwise clear view of the trees and water.

A lot of protests occurred when Carleton Industries proposed expanding its addition in the direction of the Riverwalk, but the opposition died down when the design revealed an outdoor amphitheater facing the Wahoozee River. People found it difficult to make an argument against something so beautiful that brought more culture into the community. The amphitheater is the building's only saving grace. The rest of its design creates a large blob against the skyline.

We walk in silence, each lost in thought at twilight. "Beautiful," Brian utters. For a moment, I have the gall to think he is talking about me. Then I realize he has stopped to appreciate the streaks of red near the horizon, extending sideways, until they are consumed into oblivion by the water.

Without the sun, the Riverwalk lighting is limited. We carefully make our way along the path. I point to the darkened light poles interspersed between the benches that overlook the river. "I guess someone forgot to reset the timer. The lights must still be on their daylight savings setting."

"Apparently," Brian answers. As we near my office building, he changes the subject. "I expected you to be in Chicago or D.C. by now."

"I'm here for my father. There will always be time to move on later." I don't add the obvious—that the time to move on will come when my father no longer distinguishes me from the unit nurse. "What about you? Where did you go when you graduated from the academy?"

Brian kicks at a stone before answering. "I took a job in Dover." I recognize it as a fairly big city with a lot of street crime about eighty miles west of Wahoo. "I wanted to be where the action was. Coming out of the academy, I felt eager to make the world safe using all the skills they taught us."

"And?"

"And I used them more than I ever want to again." He pauses, carefully choosing his next words. "I needed those skills whether I was on or off duty in Dover, so I was glad when Chief Johnson offered me a job on the Wahoo force." I wonder what Brian isn't telling me. I may have been out of cop-related law enforcement for the past few years, but I know going from Dover to Wahoo doesn't make sense in terms of career advancement.

"You know," Brian continues, "I'd been in Wahoo a number of times with you when we were together, and Chief Johnson and I had gotten to know each other. Even after you and I broke up, the Chief and I kept in touch. When he offered me a job here in Wahoo, it seemed like a good opportunity to work with a pro. It's been a good match-up so far, with more guys on the force like Chief Johnson than Officer Robinson."

As we reach the rear entrance to Carleton Industries, I suggest to Brian, "Why don't you wait for me at the amphitheater? My passkey lets me enter from the back, where I can ride the service elevator literally to its stopping point next to my office. The two files are sitting on my desk. It's not worth taking the time to formally check you in and out at the security desk."

"That's okay, Red. I think I have my own pass." He flips his badge at me.

My face shows my displeasure that Brian is playing his police credential trump card.

"Just kidding." He smiles broadly. "I could always get you going. I'll meet you by the amphitheater." Still chuckling to himself, he continues strolling the Riverwalk.

I'm not surprised by the lack of activity on the loading dock, but it is strange there is no guard at the rear desk. Usually guards are posted 24/7 at this desk in the basement and at each of the other entrances. A different set of guards is assigned to walk the building each hour.

Even the light by the loading dock feels dimmed. I mentally shrug and push the button for the elevator. While waiting for it I think I hear voices. I still my breathing to listen more intently. The voices seem to be coming from the basement file area that Michael and I were working in earlier today.

"B2-2," says a voice I recognize as Lester Balfour's. He's reading aloud the same words he'd read from my legal pad a few hours ago in Fourth's office. Curiosity consumes me. I move closer to the partially open door.

I hear the Fourth's distinctive tone. "Got it."

"Don't forget to move the sticker," Mr. Balfour instructs.

"I'm not an idiot, Les. I already did that. What's left on the list?"

As Mr. Balfour answers, the elevator arrives with a ping. I freeze.

"Did you hear something?" Fourth asks. I see him coming

toward the door I'm standing behind. The elevator doors slide open, but I fear cutting across the path of light spilling from the freight elevator's extra-wide opening. I don't dare pretend that I'm coming from my office, as the silence in the building and the absence of the guards makes me think that Fourth and Balfour may have given everyone the night off. I certainly don't want to get caught in a lie. Instead, I flatten myself into the shadow of the wall behind the slightly cracked door.

Fourth pushes the door open further, but not enough for it to bump into me. He peers out, but, thankfully, the only thing in his line of sight is emptiness, darkness, and the now closed elevator doors.

"Come on," Balfour commands. "You're getting jumpy. Let's get this finished. B6-4."

I don't budge. B6 is the cabinet almost next to the door. Although my view isn't as clear as it was before I backed to the wall, I can still see through the narrow strip along the hinged edge. From my vantage point, I observe Fourth open the designated drawer, pull out the stickered document and the one behind it, scan both, then move the sticker from its original place to the second document. He puts only the second document back in the drawer for copying tomorrow.

He walks back to where Lester Balfour is and hands him the now unstickered document. Balfour places it in a carton that once held ten packages of laser-printing paper. It appears almost full. He hands the carton to Fourth. "Come on, let's get this stuff into the shredder bin before everyone gets here tomorrow." I stand very still. If they come out through the loading-dock area, there's no place for me to hide.

I feel my palms sweating as I push them into the wall behind me. I force myself to think. No car was parked by the loading dock, so maybe they parked in their regular spots out front— closer to the passenger elevators. I should get so lucky.

Fourth stands right by the storage area's door as he says something else to Mr. Balfour. I hear papers rustling and realize Fourth is feeding papers into the shredder bin next to the door. I try to get a better view but keep in the shadows.

"I'd hate to be that poor schmuck when they review the documents he stickered for them," Fourth says. He lets out a deep-throated laugh that Lester cuts off by tersely ordering him to hurry up. Fourth shoves the papers more rapidly into the narrow slot. A few fall to the floor and he retrieves all but one. From my angle, I can see it has lodged itself between the wall and the shredder box.

He shakes the carton to make sure it is empty, and then turns back toward the part of the room Lester Balfour must be standing in. Fourth's rich voice continues to move away from my exposed hiding spot, but I stay glued. One of them snaps off the storage-room light.

I wait in almost total darkness, listening to make sure they are gone and not coming back. Minutes pass with me staying in the hallway's shadows. I start to inch my way to the loading-dock door. I'll use my passkey to get out, but first, feeling safe at last, I decide to retrieve the piece of paper Fourth dropped. Crouching, my head ducked down to keep my face hidden from a possible security camera, I return to the cracked door, move around it, and feel for the sheet of paper. It's too dark to read it, so I shove it into my pocket and hurry to leave, still keeping myself low to the ground. Hopefully, if there's a security camera, no one will think to review tonight's tape.

Once out on the Riverwalk, I realize I'm shaking. At least if I run into Fourth or Balfour, I can use the excuse of taking a walk. The fact that my car is parked at Sunshine Village will bolster my story, if I need one. I see Brian in the distance and I run to him, my hair flying behind me. I lean against him, still trembling.

"What's wrong, Red?" His arms instinctively embrace me as he asks again, "What's wrong? You're shaking like a leaf." I'm still processing what happened and deciding how much to tell him when we hear a scream coming from the direction of the nursing home.

My first thought is the screech is an animal in pain, but when Brian releases me and takes off running toward Sunshine Village, I realize the sound is human. I run behind him as fast as my shoes let me.

I catch up to Brian in the middle of the Riverwalk, not far from Sunshine Village's Japanese garden. He motions me to be quiet as he stands listening. For a moment, everything is so silent that all I hear is my own breathing. The next second, I hear a subdued moan coming from almost directly below the part of the path I am standing on. "Brian, here," I call to him. We both look down the rocky embankment where I am pointing. There are no more sounds and all we can see in the dimness are rocks and overgrown brush leading to the Wahoozee River.

Then I spot it.

A cane lies below us—to the side of the path where we stand. I point again. Instead of going back to one of the stairs leading to the water, Brian immediately starts down the rocky embankment. He moves quickly but carefully down the uneven terrain. I debate whether to follow him or wait to see what he finds.

I hear him stumble and curse as the lights along the Riverwalk flick on. Their unexpected glare blinds me for a moment. Until my eyes readjust, I keep staring at the dark water and trying to see Brian through the underbrush. "Go get help," he yells up to me. "Someone's down here and I've dropped my cell phone."

I pull mine out of my pocket, but it is dead; so, I turn to run up the garden path to Sunshine Village, when he calls out again. "Get an ambulance. It's Lindy Carleton."

CHAPTER EIGHTEEN

The back door to the retirement home won't open. I push on it, twist the doorknob, and give it a few hard pounds, hoping someone will hear me, but it doesn't give. My heart sinks as I realize it is after the lockdown hour. A glance at my watch confirms that the only door open for the public to enter is the main entrance, all the way around the huge building with its several wings of rooms.

I look around wildly, hoping for a way to save time. Someone must still be in the dining room or in the hallway beyond the back door, so I pound on the door again and toss gravel at the windows nearby. I think it might have been faster to run around to the front door instead of waiting for a senior citizen to slowly shuffle to the door. In my moment of panic, Barbara Balfour flings open the back door.

"Carrie? Are you okay? Your car is still in the parking lot and no one saw you leave, so we've all been so worried about you. Where have you been?"

I don't take the time to make sense of her questions, but step inside and yell, "Call an ambulance and the police!" Instead of responding, she stands there staring and throwing questions at me. People from the dining room join us, including the Mah jongg group, but Barbara doesn't do anything until I lower my voice and calmly repeat, "Please, go call an ambulance and the police. Lindy Carleton has had an accident down by the River-walk."

This time, Barbara doesn't hesitate. She sprints toward her office. I can't help noticing her skirt is dirty and there is a run in her hose. This is the first time she's ever been the least bit disheveled.

I turn to return to where I left Brian, but Mah jongg players Heidi Shapiro and Hannah Schwartz each take an arm to prevent me from leaving. "Sit down," Heidi orders. I try to pull away to see if I can help Brian or any of the staff who has gone outside, but each woman only squeezes my arms more tightly. "We need to tell you something," Heidi says.

Afraid something has happened to my father, I glance at the people now crowding together at the top of the Riverwalk, and stop struggling against Heidi and Hannah. I drop into one of the faux leather chairs strategically placed outside the dining room. The chairs are intended for those coming early for dinner to have a place to sit until the dining room opens.

The two women back away as another member of their Maj gang, tiny Karen Berger, pushes her way through. "Here, drink this," Mrs. Berger says in her surprisingly deep take-charge voice. She hands me a paper cup of water flavored with lemon. It registers with me that she was somewhere in the hallway when I arrived, but I didn't notice her going to the nearby water dispenser or returning with the cup of water. Their attention to me rather than on Lindy unnerves me.

"All of you," Mrs. Berger motions to the gathered crowd, "your food is getting cold." That quickly disperses everyone except the other Maj players back to the dining room. I take one sip of water, steeling myself for bad news about my father as Mrs. Berger demands, "Quickly, tell us where you've been."

Ella Goldring is too busy peering out the back door to pay attention to us, but Michael's mother and Hannah Schwartz, behind Karen Berger, nod solemnly. The three of them gaze at me in an odd way that I can't figure out. "Did something happen to my father?"

"No," Mrs. Berger replies. My mind immediately thinks something else has befallen Carolyn, but Mrs. Berger assures me that she is fine. "We're concerned about you. Where have you been?"

"I was on the Riverwalk with Brian and we heard a scream from the direction of Sunshine Village," I explain, now completely confused as to their behavior. "Brian realized it was a person so we ran back but didn't find anything at first. Then we heard moaning and saw a cane. Brian climbed down the embankment while I went for help."

Mrs. Berger demands, "How long were Brian and you out on the Riverwalk?"

"I don't know. A few minutes, maybe? I stopped at my office first." I'm still trying to stand up to go back to Brian—and Lindy—when we see Barbara Balfour coming back from her office.

"Carrie," Karen Berger whispers to me. "A car alarm went off about an hour ago. When it didn't stop, the receptionist went out to check and found your car window smashed. No one could find you.

"When we couldn't find you and you didn't answer your cell phone, Barbara called the police. That awful Babyface responded, so you know he will think this is more than malicious mischief, especially now with whatever has happened to Lindy."

"Look, help is already here," Ella shouts out, holding the rear door open, effectively preventing Barbara Balfour from hearing any of Mrs. Berger's whisper to me. Before I can process Karen Berger's news, I wonder if Ella is more on top of things than I gave her credit for or if her timing is merely providential. Either way, she's right.

Through the open door we see spinning red and blue lights and hear blaring sirens down by the Riverwalk. Among all my other jumbled thoughts, I know the flashing lights mean plenty of people are already on hand to help Lindy and Brian. One thing about living in a small town like Wahoo is that emergency response time is fast. It was probably even faster because Baby-face was still in the front parking lot checking out my broken window rather than at the police station.

I don't realize I'm shivering until Mrs. Schwartz tugs the pink shawl from Heidi's shoulders and wraps it around mine. The softness of the pashmina and kindness of Mrs. Schwartz is so comforting that I relax for the first time in hours. Only at this moment does Karen Berger's news about my car sink in. Someone vandalized my car, causing these nice people to be afraid something had happened to me, too.

"My father," I say aloud.

"Barbara and Marta peeked into his room," Mrs. Berger reports, "but when you weren't there, they didn't want to wake him up and upset him by asking if he knew where you were."

I nod, glad that they were that thoughtful.

"Come to think of it," Mrs. Berger says, "I better tell Carolyn you're okay. She kept hearing a car alarm going off from her room, but when she called the nurse's station to complain, no one answered. You know Carolyn. She took it upon herself to go down to the front desk to report it. When the alarm was identi-fied as coming from your car and nobody could locate you, she insisted on helping search for you until Barbara made Marta take her upstairs to lie down again."

I'm still digesting this update and wondering what someone could possibly want in my car when Ella Goldring announces, "It doesn't look good. They're bringing Lindy up way too fast." Heidi, Hannah, and Barbara cluster around Ella to get a better view of the rope and pulley system the EMTs have rigged to bring up the stretcher. "Nope, it doesn't look good at all," Ella reports to no one in particular. "I think they've got her face covered."

"Hush," Heidi admonishes her. "You can't see that clearly from here."

"Sure I can."

Maybe she can, but standing next to the group, I can't. All I can see and hear are the paramedics loading the stretcher into the ambulance and slamming its doors shut.

"Ladies, stop it," Barbara Balfour orders as the ambulance, siren on, leaves. "We'll know what's going on soon enough. They're helping Brian up the embankment now." That I can see. I hand the cup of water and the shawl back to Heidi and go out to meet him.

My heart sinks when he shakes his head at me in much the same way Marta did Sunday. "She's in pretty bad shape. Broken bones and a pretty deep gash on the back of her head. By the time I could get to her, she was going in and out of consciousness—perhaps from the pain."

Much as I'm concerned about Lindy Carleton, my attention is focused more on learning whether Brian is okay. I see scratches on his hands, probably from the brush and rocks. The seat of his pants appears as if he landed on it once too often to ever get clean again. Other than that, he seems to be in one piece physically.

"Was she able to tell you anything?"

He shakes his head again. "She tried to say something, but I couldn't understand her." Brian looks so dejected that this time I'm the one putting my arm around him. He looks at me and says, "If only I had reached her sooner or hadn't dropped my cell phone so I could call for help more quickly, maybe I could have helped her."

"Brian, no one else could have gotten down there any sooner than you did. Most people wouldn't have even realized the scream we heard was human. But for you, she could still be down there." I shudder to think of Lindy lying there among the rocks and muck. I would have continued my pep talk and asked him more questions about whether she fell or was hit, but my favorite policeman, Babyface, joins us.

He ignores me and speaks directly to Brian. "We need to cordon off the scene, sir. I already radioed Chief Johnson that, until he gets here, I'll keep this site secure, too."

"This site, too?" Brian asks.

"Yes, sir," Babyface says, finally acknowledging my presence with a nod of his head. "In the last hour or so, someone vandalized Ms. Martin's car. Broke out her front passenger window. We've been searching for her ever since we responded to the call reporting the break-in."

Now, Officer Robinson focuses his attention on me. "You certainly have an uncanny knack for being in the middle of every murder, don't you?"

"That's enough, Robinson. She's been with me."

"Yes, sir. All I'm saying is that she turns up at the most interesting times."

Brian shoots him a look, but I'm not sure if it even registers with Babyface. "We're going to need to notify Ms. Carleton's son and granddaughter, get the techs out here to take some pictures, and . . ."

"No problem, sir. I've already called for the techs and Chief Johnson is going to run point with the family. I need to take your statement, as well as Ms. Martin's, sir."

"Don't you think you're overstepping your bounds a bit, Officer Robinson?"

"No, sir. Not in a small town like ours," he said, puffing his chest out. "We don't worry so much about rank as getting the job done."

Brian starts to point out a procedural point, but Babyface

smiles and cuts him off. "Detective McPhillips," he says, once again referring to Brian formally, "you of all people must realize the importance of appearance to any investigation. It would be a matter of impropriety, reflecting badly on Chief Johnson, for you to be part of this murder investigation."

"Murder? You keep referring to *this* as a murder investigation. All I've heard so far is that someone broke into my car and we know that Lindy has been hurt."

This time, Babyface is happy to acknowledge my presence. "Yes, Ms. Martin. Murder. Chief Johnson doesn't want to announce it until we can notify her son, but Lindy Carleton was dead, probably from the blow to the back of her head, before we put her in the ambulance."

CHAPTER NINETEEN

Even with Babyface reined in by Chief Johnson, it takes almost two hours for Brian and me to give our separate statements, re-enact where we were when we heard Lindy scream and demonstrate how each of us responded. At 10 p.m., when I think we are done with this exercise, Babyface insists we examine the damage to my car.

"Not a problem," I snap. "Where else do you think I'm about to go? I only hope you secured that scene as well as you did this one." I point to all the yellow tape strung around the Riverwalk and the edge of Sunshine Village's Japanese garden.

As Brian, Babyface and I round the edge of the building, I look around for Chief Johnson. I believe things would go more smoothly with him on the scene, but he's probably still interviewing Barbara Balfour or consoling the recently located Carleton IV.

It seems impossible that only four hours have passed since Brian and I opted to go for dinner. Events blur in my mind, but my churning feelings cannot erode the clarity of my mother and Lindy's deaths. Brian's whistle, when we spot my car, interrupts my thoughts.

Shards of glass cover the ground next to the passenger side door. "You gotta be kidding," I say. "There's nothing in my car anyone could want."

The words barely leave my mouth when Brian and I look at each other. We run to the car, making sure not to touch anything as we peer through the broken window. The glove compartment door hangs wide open. My leather gloves, a map, my car registration, a few McDonald's straws and sunglasses are strewn on the seat and floor. I can see the piece of pipe cleaner stuck on the edge of the plastic door, but there is no sign of the envelope my mother gave me.

CHAPTER TWENTY

The few days after Lindy's death pass quickly. On Tuesday, the glass-repair people vacuum up the remaining bits of glass in my car and install a new window. My father is as he always has been—no better but no worse. I catch up at the office, but don't feel it necessary to find out if the discovery documents are copied and delivered by close of business Wednesday. For me, that is the day my mother is buried with just my father, Brian, Carolyn, and me in attendance. On Thursday, CI shuts down for three hours so that our mandatory attendance at Lindy's funeral overflows the church.

I work hard at not dwelling on my mother's murder or what might have been in the letter. I also can't forget what I saw in CI's basement on Monday night. Thoughts of my giving the location list to Fourth and Mr. Balfour and then seeing them shredding the documents Michael marked constantly intrude on whatever I am doing. I think about taking the page I retrieved to Brian or Michael and telling them what happened, because it is the right thing to do, but I need my job. My father would tell me to act with integrity and to think about whether my silence might harm Michael and Molly, but keeping my father at Sunshine Village requires a part of my monthly wages. I compensate by spending more time with him.

I try to avoid most of the Sunshine Village residents, especially the Mah jongg players, because their favorite topic of speculation is a variation of who, how, and why my mother and Lindy

Carleton were killed.

During one of my visits to the retirement home, Molly reminds me that her Nana always has Shabbat dinner on Friday at six, no matter what time sundown really is. So, here I am, in the hall outside Heidi Shapiro's apartment, wondering if I should be bringing a bottle of Manischewitz wine instead of the extra bottle of Merlot I had in my apartment.

I am uncomfortable because I've never attended a Shabbat dinner and because I haven't seen Michael since Monday night's raid on his marked discovery documents. Facing him, without confessing the truth, is going to be very difficult for me. Because the thought of lying to him makes me nauseous, I dread being in the same room making small talk with him.

Molly barely gives me time to knock before she flings open the door and announces my arrival. Heidi, her pink blouse and capri pants covered by a red-and-white-checkered apron reading "Eat At Your Own Risk," gives me a kiss and relieves me of my wine.

"Michael," she shouts across the apartment, "Carrie is here! She brought a bottle of wine. Would you open it so we can all have some?" Noticing Molly's excited look, Heidi corrects herself. "All except you, my dear. You may pour yourself some grape juice."

"But Nana," Molly protests. Heidi, smiling, shakes her head no. Molly is so dejected, I ask for grape juice, too. Maybe I'm subconsciously protecting myself from doing something stupid tonight. I feel so awkward being here with Michael, but I don't have to worry for long about saying something stupid.

Michael ignores me and busies himself opening the wine. I greet the other guests, the rest of the Mah jongg players. They are sitting at the card table in the corner of the room stacking tiles, two high, along the entire length of the four brightly colored plastic racks as if building Great Walls of China. Apparently, they plan an after-dinner game. Heidi leaves them to their wall building and returns to the kitchen area. I tag along behind her.

Eventually, she accepts my offer to help by letting me fill the glasses on the table with ice cubes and water. Heidi doesn't have an automatic ice dispenser. Instead, I get the cubes from old-fashioned metal trays stacked in her freezer. The trays are no problem for me to manipulate. Growing up, that was the job the ladies auxiliary let me do for all of my father's church socials. As I pour water into the final glass, Heidi invites us to join her at the table.

I hold back from taking a chair, wondering where to sit, but Molly grabs my hand. "Come on," she says, tugging at me. "You're sitting between Daddy and me."

Everyone quickly sits except Heidi and Michael. She stands on one side of the table in front of two candleholders, a small bit of lace on her head. Lighting each of the candles, she lays the spent match on the table, covers her eyes, and then rotates her hands while intoning a blessing in another language. When she finishes, she sits down.

Michael holds a silver chalice up high, in front of his face. He says a prayer, in what I guess is Hebrew, and then, whether this is for my benefit or something he does regularly, he recites in English, "Blessed art thou, O Lord our God, King of the Universe, creator of the fruit of the vine." As Michael raises the glass to his lips, everyone, except me, timely chants "Amen."

He puts the wine glass down and tears a chunk off the twisted bread in front of him. Breaking off a smaller piece from the chunk, he passes the rest around so each of us can hold a small piece of challah. Once he is satisfied no one is without bread, he offers a second prayer in Hebrew and then in English. "Blessed art thou, O Lord our God, King of the Universe, who brings forth bread from the earth." This time, I join everyone in saying

"Amen" and eating the pieces of bread in our hands.

Heidi and Karen Berger quickly rise from their chairs to serve each of us chicken noodle soup. From the pieces of chicken and the plentiful, thin, egg noodles, I know one of these women has made the soup from scratch rather than merely opening a can. My bet is on Mrs. Berger, the queen of chocolate marble cake. Yet, Heidi apparently hosts Shabbat dinner each week.

Michael seems to read my mind. He leans over to tell me, "Ever since they were all widowed, they've sort of created their own family. My mother has the largest apartment, so dinner usually is here, but all of the Maj players help. Brisket made with Coca-Cola is Mom's specialty, but Karen always makes the soup and a dessert. Hannah takes care of the vegetables and Ella used to make the salad, but now she orders it sent up from the kitchen downstairs."

I am grateful to Michael for the explanation and for easing the tension between us. Relieved that the awkwardness of the evening has passed, I ask, "And the bread?"

"Store-bought challah, though all of them know how to make it. When I was little, they often made their weekly Friday-night challahs together, teaching us kids how to roll and braid tubular pieces of dough so the final product would be a twisted challah." He adds, "Knowing how to braid comes in handy when Molly doesn't want to wear a ponytail."

Molly is lucky Michael can braid hair. My father had many skills, but doing hair wasn't one of them. After untangling my hair once too many times, he had Carolyn take me to a beauty shop where they cut it pixie style. I hated it that short so I learned how to do it without my father's help.

Together, Michael and I watch Molly, who stands by the buffet, which is larger than my office credenza. She is making sure each of the main dishes that Heidi placed on the buffet has a serving utensil. When Heidi gives the high sign for everyone to go through the line, I hold back, but Michael ushers me in front of him. "You're company." I don't need to be told twice, because everything looks delicious.

I sit down anticipating good food and the glass of Merlot that Michael replaced my grape juice with.

"So, Carrie," Ella Goldring says, pausing to swallow a bite of noodle kugel. "Who do you think killed your mother and Lindy?"

I almost choke on my wine. I'm not sure I even hear her correctly because in the next breath, she compliments Mrs. Schwartz on how light her kugel is.

"Now, Ella, we don't know if the same person killed both of them," Heidi observes, helping herself to two slices of brisket. "Do we, Carrie?"

All eyes, except Michael's, turn to me. He throws his hands up in the air. "Mom! We're having Shabbat dinner."

"So, we're not allowed to talk while we eat?"

Michael glares at his mother as she continues.

"The girls and I have been giving it a lot of thought, and we can't decide if the same person killed both of them." She waits for me to say something.

"The police haven't been keeping me in the loop for either of their investigations, Mrs. Shapiro." I sample the brisket.

"Heidi," she says. "Call us by our first names. If you don't, we'll know you can't remember them." As the other women nod, she again asks if I think the same person killed my mother and Lindy.

"Those determinations are best left to the professionals." I try not to sound condescending. Michael stares at his mother.

"Hogwash." Ella peers over the top of her glasses at me. "If we've all been thinking about it, I know you've been wondering, too." When I still don't take the bait, she peeks at Heidi and Karen.

Karen takes a sip of water. "Carrie, you aren't the only one we want to help here. We live here. We've got a personal interest in finding out what happened to your mother, to Carolyn, and to Lindy. You heard Lindy complaining about food and feeling like a prisoner. We don't feel like prisoners . . ."

"The food could be better," Ella interjects.

". . . but at the moment we don't feel completely safe, either." Karen ignores Ella's interruption. "We don't trust Officer Robinson to help us anymore than he did with Hannah's issue last year. If anything, his unwillingness to listen made everything worse."

"If it wasn't for Michael, I'd probably still be in jail," Hannah says, giving him a look of pure adoration. "I was guilty of keying the Nazi's car, you know."

Michael clears his throat and loosens his tie. "I really didn't do anything. There turned out to be some extenuating circumstances that made negotiation and dismissal of the suit and countersuit amenable to all parties."

Karen puts her wine glass down firmly on the table, the noise catching everyone's attention. "We can't trust Babyface to do the right thing by any of us. Although we know Detective McPhillips is your friend, we're having our doubts about him, too."

I'm surprised to hear her say that. Unless he has changed drastically, Brian is a good detective and a good man. "We've talked it over," she says, waving her hand toward me and the other Mah jongg players, "and think that all of us could be a pretty powerful investigative team. Our skill sets complement each other well."

"Everyone at Sunshine Village knows us," Hannah adds, "so we can move about the building and grounds easily." Her enthusiasm is dampened when Karen glares at her and then resumes control of their argument.

"We don't have your police training and legal background," Karen says. "But, you could guide us so that at Sunshine Village we could be your eyes and ears."

"I don't think that would be a very good idea." Fearing that I have insulted Karen, I hastily continue talking. "What I mean is that when I was at the police academy, we were taught how much better it is when civilians, like us, don't interfere. They even called our lecture 'Dealing with Miss Marple and Other Public Pests.' That's why I've trusted Brian to do his job and deliberately not asked too many questions about the investigation of my mother's death."

"Compare it to playing Mah Jongg," Heidi says, ignoring my rationale. "You have to know that the tiles are divided into craks, dots, bams, winds, flowers, and jokers, but it takes skill, like you have from the academy, to decide which hand the tiles best match. If you pick a closed hand and your tile goes by, you can't help yourself. If you pick an open hand and call, you have to expose some of your tiles, which lets everyone play a little more defensively against you. It's the same as figuring out these crimes—a delicate balance of what you know, what you can find out, and luck."

"I don't know what . . ."

"Carrie," Molly interrupts, "how come you didn't know the lady in Ms. Holt's room was your mother?"

"Honey," Hannah says, "the lady's hat and coat covered her face. None of us knew it wasn't Carolyn."

"I would have known my mother," Molly assures us. She opens her little purse, peers at a small picture of her mother, and then looks at me expectantly. There's really nothing I can say that will ease this moment for Molly. I wish I could turn time back to before the Mah jongg players and I began this conversation. We are so wrapped up in our cares and worries at Sunshine Village that we treat Molly as one of us, forgetting to be sensitive to her needs as a child.

As Molly snaps her purse closed, Heidi breaks the silence by beginning to clear the dishes. I hurry to help, but leaning forward to pick up a soup bowl, I stop. "I should have known my mother," I tell Molly and everyone else in the room. "I'd seen her only a few hours earlier so I should have remembered she wore jeans and sneaks."

No one interrupts me, but I can tell from the Mah jongg group's faces that they aren't following my logic. "After all the times I've seen Carolyn in her Halloween costume, I should have instinctively realized something was off when I didn't see her Burberry boots," I explain. "My memory antenna didn't go off."

Heidi puts the stack of plates she holds down on the table. "But it should have," she says. "That's why we think we can help you and you can help us figure this out. We bring different perspectives to the table.

My mind goes back to those first few moments in Room 346. Slowly, it dawns on me. "Probably for the same reason Mrs. Schwartz, I mean Hannah, also assumed it was Carolyn. It was her room and she was wearing the Burberry coat and hat. Moreover, both women were about the same size and shape."

"That's right," Hannah says.

"But something felt wrong in that room, but I couldn't figure it out. Nothing jumped out at me to make me think it wasn't Carolyn or to give me an 'I know this person' sensation. In fact, it didn't occur to me until now that I should have noticed the jeans and sneakers."

I remind myself to review the pictures on my phone, which I've almost forgotten I'd taken. Maybe there are other things I didn't see when I was in the room. Now that I have a little time and distance from the moment, maybe I can spot something I missed.

"Marta and I didn't notice the jeans and boots were wrong, either," Hannah observes. "But, Marta should have when she put her hands on the wrist and neck to see if the woman was still breathing."

I hadn't realized Marta touched the body. The hat and coat didn't appear disrupted to me. Maybe Marta pulled the brim down, and, if so, why?

Heidi and I are each lost in thought as we resume clearing the table. I place my second round of dishes on the counter near the sink when Heidi orders me back to the dining room. "There isn't enough space for more than two of us in here and Karen and I have a method." Heidi bobs her head toward Karen, who is scraping a plate into the trashcan.

I fully understand Heidi's preference for Karen's help. Secretly, I'm relieved to be off kitchen duty. As a child, I was sent to play by the women at the church as they cleaned up from church functions, and as an adult, I have always felt more comfortable talking with the men after dinner than with the women. Consequently, unless I make a conscious effort to remember to help, I tend to be oblivious when cleanup begins. I have to remind myself, at the first opportunity, to jump up to clear, so that if I should become engaged in a conversation, no one can later accuse me of being too good for kitchen duties.

"Until we make enough room to serve dessert," Heidi suggests, "why don't you and Michael go out on the patio where you won't be underfoot?" Michael looks as uncomfortable as I am with the idea, but we are stuck with it, especially when even Molly joins in pushing us out on the patio.

For the second time in a week, I am with an eligible man

watching the sunset. Hopefully, even though I feel weighed down by my guilt, this sunset viewing won't prove as deadly as the last one.

Chapter Twenty-One

The big difference watching the sunset with Michael is that I know he has no interest in making any moves on me. Even if he tried, I'm too ashamed to respond appropriately. I sit in one of Heidi's deck chairs as we use the sunset for a topic of conversation. After he comments on its lovely rose shade tonight, I respond that the roses in the garden are an equally lovely hue. When I look at his face in the fading moments of sunlight, I realize what I have said. "I'm so sorry. I didn't mean to upset you by talking about the garden. I forgot your wife . . ."

"It's okay. The roses are lovely." He puts his hands on the railing and faces the garden, his back to me. "Molly hates this garden now. She won't go near it. And I'm sure you've noticed how she always has a little purse."

I mutter, "Yes."

"She's allergic to bee stings, too, so she won't go anywhere without having a epi pen with her at all times." He glances toward the edge of the Japanese garden near the trees. "I know I should hate this garden, but its very beauty reminds me of Jess. Sometimes I bring a book and sit over there." He points and I get up to see exactly what he is pointing at. It is a delicate redwood bridge with stones piled into walls on either side of it. "I sit there with my book, except I never turn a page. I just think about Jess."

He keeps his face pointed to the garden, even as I put my hand on his arm. "You must have loved her very much."

"I still do." Michael then becomes quiet. Once again, I have the sense to know this is a silence that doesn't need filling. When we hear Molly's laugh from inside the apartment, we turn to catch her dancing with Ella.

"Molly is the best thing Jess and I ever did," Michael reports with satisfaction. "Jess and I met when our parents put us in the same Hebrew-school carpool."

I murmur a sound so he knows I'm listening.

"Both of our families were pleased when we got married— nice Jewish boy marries nicer Jewish girl. That was a big thing for our families, but not as big as when Molly came along two years later. That let our mothers brag about their nice Jewish lawyer son who could afford to let their nice Jewish daughter stay at home with their perfect Jewish granddaughter with her perfect nose."

I must have a quizzical expression. "Molly got my nose instead of the one her mom got fixed by a plastic surgeon when she was eighteen." Michael forces a laugh, but when he faces me, I'm pretty sure his eyes are moist. "I loved Jess just as much with her original nose. My only fear was that I wasn't good enough for her and Molly."

"That's ridiculous."

"No, Jess's mother wanted her to marry a doctor."

"Oh, come on. Now you're pulling my leg with a stereotypical joke."

"Honest Injun," he says with a straight face. "Jess's mother wanted Jess to marry her best friend's son, Jeffrey Tenebaum, so she could say she had a doctor as a son-in-law, and that Mrs. Tenebaum and she were truly sisters."

"But," I point out, "she married you."

"That she did." He smiles. "Jess said it was because she couldn't imagine a lifetime of being touched by someone who ate his own boogers when they were in playgroup."

"Surely he outgrew that phase of his life before medical school."

"She wasn't sure, but since he became a pathologist, we figured it didn't much matter."

Though what Michael said isn't that amusing, the image of a booger-eating pathologist strikes me as downright funny and I can't help but laugh. Neither can Michael. I try to get myself under control, but when we look at each other, we each burst out laughing again. Soon any tears on either of our faces are from laughter, not sorrow.

I want to tell him how sorry I am for the loss of his young wife, the loss of Molly's mother, but I can't find the words. Luckily, I don't have to, because Molly calls us in for dessert. All the Maj players are seated around the table, Cheshire-cat grins on their faces. Either they think the cake Karen is about to cut is exceptional or they are reacting to the laughter they heard coming from the patio.

CHAPTER TWENTY-TWO

Leaving Heidi's apartment, I realize it still is early enough for me to visit my father. To my surprise, he is in bed for the night, but Carolyn sits on the edge of his bed in her nightgown and robe. They are playing cards. "Ah," she says, holding her cards close to her chest. "You've caught us at our regular guilty pleasure."

My father nods. "We play every night. Carolyn says nothing is as relaxing as a game of cards before bed."

She smiles. "My mother used to tell me that. Her name was Deborah, which means busy as a bee and she was a whirlwind. But, no matter how busy she was, she listened to me read a chapter aloud each night and then we played a game of cards before bed. I always sleep soundly after playing, especially if I win."

I make a mental note to tease my father later, when we are alone. When I was a kid, he'd have me recite my prayers every night before bed and then, as he tucked my comforter around me, he'd tell me there was nothing that made sleep easier than opening one's heart to God. I had to agree because I slept like a log once I told God everything bad that happened that day and asked God to bless everyone I knew, naming each person.

I can't remember how many times I confessed to getting in trouble with Carolyn for talking too loudly or running at the library, but I would always make sure to ask God to bless her, thinking that would even everything out. In retrospect, I'm not sure how my father kept a straight face listening to my prayers.

Apparently cards now outweigh prayer as the means of guaranteeing restful sleep. With my worries about my father and my frustration that Brian doesn't seem to be doing much toward finding out who killed my mother, maybe I should take up solitaire. It would probably be healthier for me than wine.

"With your week," I kid Carolyn, "I would think you'd be tired enough tonight to not need anything to relax you."

"I am, but I'm never too tired to beat your father at gin rummy. Gin!" she announces, laying down her cards face-up on the bedspread. They laugh. Carolyn gathers the cards and puts them back in the box sitting on my father's nightstand. "Besides, I want to make sure Peter sleeps well, too. It's important for him that we stick to our rituals." As Carolyn bends down and gives my father a quick kiss on his head, I think about the crush she supposedly has on him but it dawns on me that the kiss and her reference to the need to reinforce rituals is because of his Alzheimers.

My father doesn't kiss her back, but he beams happily.

"Good night, Peter. Better luck tomorrow night." As she walks by me on her way out of the room, she gives me a hug. "And good night to you, too."

After she goes, I take her seat on my father's bed. His expression changes from utter relaxation to a more serious one as he asks, "What's the matter, Carrie?"

I want to tell him everything that happened this week, but I know I can't burden him with the issues from work.

"Is it Charlotte?"

At the mention of her name, I nod and wait for him to speak.

"She told me that she told you everything and gave you the letter. So, what is it that's bothering you?"

Haltingly, I tell my father how I couldn't get beyond the letter's opening, why I saved it to read later, and why I probably will never have an opportunity to read it. I bring him up to date on what she told me about why she left him, and how I tried to talk to him later that day but he was out of his head from the urinary infection. Once again, I feel tears welling in my eyes. Normally, I don't show my emotions, but the events of this week have brought my deepest feelings and fears to the surface.

"I can't tell you how much I've wanted to be able to talk to you about what the letter was about and if you have any idea who might have stolen it." I hesitate because I don't want to mention that I couldn't ask him because his periods of lucidity were so fleeting. I don't want to upset him. Instead, I simply say, "but the timing hasn't been right."

My father leans forward to hold me close to him. For the first time I notice the nursing-home scent of disinfectant soap about him instead of the sweet smell of aftershave.

"Carrie, your mother was a good woman. She loved you very much."

I bury my head in his shoulder before I mutter, "But she left me. She could have taken me with her. Instead, she abandoned me."

"No, she left you with me. To take you away from me and everything you had known would have been, in her mind, to abandon you." He nudges me away from him so our eyes meet. "Your mother never abandoned you," he declares. "She loved you until the moment she died."

"I don't understand."

"Your mother knew when she left me she was choosing a difficult life. She didn't want that for you. She weighed what she felt I could give you against what she feared she couldn't give you." Now it's my father's turn to question what he believed. His face grows serious and tired. "I know we've had our differences, but it hasn't been that bad, has it?"

"No," I assure him. Even when I questioned my father's

church and faith, rebelled by partying too much and not acting like a perfect minister's kid, or the times I did exactly the opposite of what he wanted or approved of in my professional and personal lives, I knew I could always count on him to love me unconditionally.

"My letter," he says as he lies back on his pillows, exhausted from our limited conversation.

He starts to finish his thought, but I put my finger to his lips. "Later. You can tell me what was in the letter, tomorrow." Content, my father closes his eyes. I sit with him, as he used to do with me, until he falls asleep.

The biggest difference in our role reversal is that when I was a child, he heard my prayers, read me a story, and waited for me to fall asleep dreaming of happy things. Tonight, I am not content. My questions about why, within only hours of her coming back into my life, my mother was killed, or what is in the letter, remain unanswered. They need to wait for another night or until, on my own, I figure out exactly what happened to her on Sunday, from the time she left my office until she was killed.

CHAPTER TWENTY-THREE

Even though Brian called and invited me to meet him, I assure myself it's not a date if he doesn't pick me up. My left brain challenges my right brain that I'm acting delusional. Checking my makeup once more and applying lipstick, I realize my left brain is correct. For me to put on makeup and intentionally meet Brian on a Saturday night at the FattBurger cannot be passed off as two old friends simply deciding to get together to catch up. Then again, that sounds better than saying I have a date with the detective investigating my mother's murder.

I drive myself to the FattBurger and, as always, it's packed. I'm right on time, yet Brian apparently has been here for a while. He not only has a table, but also a partially finished beer in front of him.

"Starting without me?"

Sliding into my side of the booth, the one facing the wall, I notice a second half-consumed beer on the table. When Brian glances over my left shoulder, I turn to see what caught his eye. I am so surprised to see Michael I almost miss Brian saying, "When he called me, I thought it might be a good idea for the three of us to talk." Michael sits down next to me and pulls his beer closer to him.

"Would you like something?" he asks, signaling to catch the waitress's attention. Hemmed in by him, I decide not to make a scene by trying to leave. Instead, I order a sweet tea. When the waitress leaves with my drink order, Michael wastes no time getting to the point of our meeting. "I was fired this afternoon."

Because Brian is watching me, I feign shock. "Why?"

"They said I was incompetent. That I couldn't even handle routine discovery." He stares at me, but I don't respond. I'm surprised Michael doesn't act more upset. I would if I was fired.

Brian presses Michael for details.

"I had all the academic credentials to be hired by G&D— undergrad with honors from the University of Michigan and top of my 'Bama' law-school class. I did state and federal judicial clerkships and, more importantly to G&D, my family was and is pretty well connected in Wahoo."

I nod, remembering that Michael's late father not only ran a business, but was also on the school board for many years. Heidi and both of his grandmothers' names, when they were alive, regularly appeared in the *Wahoo Times* either for being at some social gathering or chairing a charitable event.

"I admit," he says, playing with his almost-empty beer mug, "I never became the shining star the firm expected. I don't—I mean *didn't*—particularly care for most of our corporate-law practice, but I never slacked off or did anything to be considered incompetent."

The waitress brings my drink and takes our food orders. As I tear the paper from my straw, I can't help but ask Michael the same question that a lot of young lawyers, including me, ask ourselves: "Would you want to go back with the firm or what would you rather be doing?"

"I'm not sure," Michael answers. "But I've a few months of severance pay to figure that out." He drinks about a third of a newly arrived beer that I didn't see him order. His second that I know of. "I like working with people who need my help."

Before he can elaborate, Brian steers him back to his dismissal.

"I admit the firm could rightfully have canned me after my first few years as not being a good fit or rainmaker but they were afraid it would reflect badly on them because of my family's ties to the Jewish and civic communities. I probably should have had the guts to leave when I knew I wasn't partnership material, but I was married, had a child, and we'd built a lifestyle around that fat paycheck. Instead of quitting or being fired, the firm and I had a polite meeting of the minds. I agreed that instead of being on the partnership track, I'd be a well-salaried contract attorney who'd oversee the collections department and occasionally do other duties as assigned."

So, before his presence at CI confused me, I originally was right thinking he was head of the collections department. "How could you be on contract and head of the collections department?"

"Easy. G&D classified me as a contract attorney, but I managed the daily operations of the collections department instead of practicing law." Brian makes a noise Michael takes as a request for further clarification.

"When G&D began, work was slow so they started a collections service. They got contracts with some of the local department stores to recover outstanding accounts receivable. We do it the same way today that G&D did it then. Women with scripts staff the phones either demanding payment or working out payment plans. Every time they get a payment or payment plan, G&D takes half the amount recovered."

"Pretty profitable if the volume is high," Brian says.

"You've got it," Michael acknowledges. "The firm has fifty-four women working in its collections department." I let out a low whistle and question where G&D hides that many people. I've been to the firm a few times and the décor is pretty standard. There are a few conference and copy or break rooms, but otherwise the halls are office after office of lawyers and paralegals. The only way to tell them apart is that secretaries sit outside the lawyers' offices.

"Most lawyers frown on having this type of work associated with their firms, but G&D embraces it. They've dedicated the entire basement floor to collections because they realize the department essentially covers overhead and gives attorneys the freedom to build up practices in areas they prefer to work in. I got the job because just about the time we were negotiating my contract-lawyer status, the guy who'd headed the department for many years retired. It seemed a win-win for me to do both collections and help out as needed."

"But you were at Carleton Industries on Monday," I prompt.

"One of those 'other duties as assigned.' The lead litigator—the other guy who came with me on Monday, but didn't stay—thought it was beneath him to mark documents for a pro-bono or charity case. Because I did a most of the background work on the case, the powers that be figured I would be more efficient than a first-year clerk, so I got the assignment to read and mark."

He shakes his head, then drains his beer and signals for a refill. "The partners who fired me today informed me, 'marking discovery documents doesn't take a genius to distinguish pertinent documents from irrelevant memos.' I know my concentration level has dropped a bit since Jess died, but not to this degree. I don't understand what happened. Do you?" Michael looks at me when he asks this question, but I treat it as rhetorical. I can't let my job go down the drain, too.

The waitress brings our three FattBurger specials and Michael's beer. I immediately bite into mine, but Brian doesn't pick up his burger so he can ask Michael another question. "When you called me today, you said you thought there might be a connection between Lindy Carleton's death and you being fired. From what you've said so far, I don't see how the two tie together."

Michael takes a swig of his beer. "Lindy was a complainer," he begins. "A kvetch. She found fault, but she tried to improve things. She was the type of woman who, if you said the sky was blue, would squint at it and tell you it was a haze caused by damage to the ozone layer."

"I could see her saying that." I take another bite from my burger.

"Yes, but what most people don't know is that she wouldn't stop there. She'd put a group together to save the ozone layer. Truth be told, Lindy Carleton was a bleeding heart conservationist."

"Over-made-up, beehive hair, and over-jeweled are things I might have expected to hear about Lindy Carleton," Brian says, "but Lindy Carleton, tree-hugger?"

"Major hugger." Michael points out the window. "She's the main reason we have the Riverwalk."

I wash down my FattBurger with my iced tea. "I never heard of her being involved with the Riverwalk. I grew up in this town, and know of her work with the Carleton Theater and the arts, but I don't remember her as being particularly charitable beyond the arts."

"That's how she wanted it." Michael pushes his beer aside and leans closer to me. I try to move away, but there isn't much more room for me to slide on the bench seat. "It goes back to her interpretation of *Pollyanna* and *Magnificent Obsession.*"

Both Brian and I are now absolutely confused and wondering if it's Michael or the beer talking.

"Very simple," he says. "When James Carleton III fell for Lindy, she was an aspiring actress who'd failed in New York but ended up a featured showgirl. When he brought her home to meet his parents, needless to say, they were anything but thrilled.

It took time for them to warm up to her. They went through the motions of hosting a formal wedding and reception for them at the Oakwood Church. She won them over when they finally understood she loved their son, was bright, and was willing to let James III's mother tutor her on manners, speech, and community responsibility. The Carleton Theater and Lindy's formal patronage of the arts came from their realization that regardless of what they did to change her image, they'd never get the showgirl completely out of her. Their endowment of the Carleton Theater gave her an acceptable creative outlet."

"Something she could headline every season?"

"Only in the beginning. The first few seasons, she associated her name with everything she did, but after she starred as Aunt Polly in a production of *Pollyanna,* she took to heart the lesson Polly learns—that people come to hate it when your name is on everything. About the same time, she read *Magnificent Obsession* and embraced the concept that by giving anonymously, the good comes back to you to give again. From then on, she did everything in Wahoo without fanfare."

"Such as?" Brian's full attention is definitely captured.

"Well, for example, after she gave birth to the 'Fourth,' she had the Carleton Foundation expand the public library to include a children's wing, and she endowed the funds to pay for a separate children's librarian. She actually paid Carolyn Holt's salary for years."

"Funny," I observe. "As much time as I spent with Carolyn at the library while growing up, I never knew Lindy Carleton was involved with the children's wing."

"The same is true of her spearheading the building of the Riverwalk. She felt the shoreline should be protected from commercial development and pollution."

"But Michael," I object, "the CI building is the single eyesore on the Riverwalk."

"That last expansion was the Fourth's doing over the objections of his mother. With her help, the nonprofit Public Trust Group represented by G&D fought him and Lester Balfour on their expansion plans. The best we could get as a concession to Lindy was the amphitheater."

"I don't remember reading her name in the paper when the fight was going on."

"You didn't, Carrie. The Public Trust group that my firm— that is, ex-firm—does pro-bono work for was the public face. She fed us information behind the scenes. I got to know her working on the case."

Brian reaches across the table for catsup for his fries. "Why would she feed you information to use against her son and her own retirement interests?"

"Simple. Fourth and his mother didn't see eye-to-eye. She thought he was a money-loving grub who took environmental shortcuts for the sake of a few extra bucks." Brian and I exchange glances as Michael continues. "She was right, of course. But rather than give in, he spent the last year or two spreading the word that she was a doddering dingbat."

I can't help but think of the things I heard about her when she moved into Sunshine Village. They fit what Michael describes as the anti-Lindy campaign, the opposite of the Lindy I met in Mrs. Shapiro's apartment. "So, Fourth took advantage of her fall by sticking her in Sunshine Village?"

"Yes. He tried to discredit her, and it nearly worked, but Lindy was feisty and smarter than her son. She worked hard to walk again. Everyone thought it was part of her recovery to take twice daily strolls on the Riverwalk, but what none of them knew, especially him, was that her walks let her assess firsthand what was going on with the river. She's the one who first got the pictures of the dead fish for G&D's lawsuit and brought it to the media's attention."

I'm shocked that Lindy took the pictures and made them public. It took a lot of guts for her to go public against her own son and personal interests.

"Well and good that she was a conservationist," Brian says, "but what you're telling me doesn't make total sense. Why didn't she change things in the company rather than going public and hurting her own bottom-line investment?"

"Lindy liked what money could buy her, but she felt she had more than enough to sustain her lifestyle. She didn't think it would hurt her son to have a little less. I think she hoped if he did the right thing for the river, it might make him a more responsible man. When she realized he and Lester Balfour didn't plan to change anything, and that the river could be irreparably damaged, she contacted me and made arrangements to leave Sunshine Village."

"If what you're saying is true, why didn't she move immediately?"

"She felt some of the practices at Sunshine Village might be on the shady side so she got it in her head to stay and dig a little deeper for the sake of those who couldn't leave. Plus, with the trial coming up, Lindy wanted to be near the Riverwalk in case she saw any other instances of pollution. The discovery I was involved with was the last step before the fight pitting her against Carleton IV and Lester Balfour for control of the company was scheduled to begin."

"Where does Balfour come into this?" Brian asks.

"Les Balfour provided legal advice to James Carleton III when he expanded the company. Later, Les assumed day-to-day operations of one of the subsidiaries. Fourth made him a senior VP. From everything we've been doing with the Riverwalk project, I've come to the conclusion that Balfour answers only to himself and the God of greenbacks."

For the first time, I regret Wahoo has lost Lindy. This isn't the same woman who terrorized the staff and residents of Sunshine Village. Then again, for her to accomplish the things Michael describes would require a lot of drive, personal strength, and probably the ability to be somewhat controlling behind the scenes.

Sitting with Michael and Brian, I'm torn between the attorney–client privilege that exists because of being CI's legal representative while Michael was marking the documents and my inclination to tell them everything about Monday night. Surely, even if the document I picked up is privileged, what I observed in the basement wouldn't be protected by the attorney–client privilege—only by my own "I need this job" provision.

My decision is made for me by a woman's voice. "You three look like an unholy alliance. What are you up to?" I turn to see Barbara Balfour behind our booth. Her father stands rigidly next to her.

"Probably the same thing as the two of you." Brian points at his almost untouched hamburger special. "We decided to ditch the dining room at Sunshine Village for a FattBurger. What's your excuse?"

Barbara laughs as the pager in her hand flashes a series of red lights. "Saved from confessing!" She waves her pager at the hostess. As she follows her dad to their table, she calls to us over her shoulder, "Enjoy your dinner."

Once they are beyond earshot, Brian waits expectantly for me to make a comment, but the moment has passed. I rethink Brian's deficiency in math. He's missed the equation that:

1 employer who sees the detective investigating his nemesis's murder + 1 lawyer recently fired for bungling discovery at that employer's company + 1 lawyer who made it possible for that discovery to be tampered with, may = 1 fired lawyer who desperately needs her job.

CHAPTER TWENTY-FOUR

Michael and Brian each had parked in the FattBurger's front lot, but Brian insists on walking me to my car in the rear overflow lot. As the Riverwalk comes into view, he asks me if I'd like to finish our stroll. "No," I answer too quickly. "After what happened to Lindy, I'm not sure I'll ever enjoy this part of the Riverwalk again."

"What's really going on, Red?"

"Nothing." I reach for my Honda's front door handle, but Brian slips between my car and me.

"Red, it doesn't take a detective to know something is bothering you." Unable to answer him, I stare at the water. He follows my gaze, but stops when his eyes rest on the part of Carleton Industries that juts out toward the shoreline. "You were pretty upset when you came out of the building the other night. Does it have something to do with Michael and the discovery documents he got fired over?"

"Are you kidding?" I say, hoping to distract him. The last thing I want him to remember is that when I ran to him at the amphitheater, I wasn't holding anything.

"What happened when you were in the building?"

"Nothing. Nothing that impacts any of the ongoing investigations."

Brian moves back so the light from the restaurant's neon sign puts him in the shadows while forcing me to stand where it reflects on my face. "You saw something that night, didn't you?"

113

"I don't want to talk about that night." I step away from him, hoping to get to my car and out of the harsh light.

He again pushes me to tell him what happened, but stops in mid-sentence, slapping his head. "How stupid can I be? You saw something having to do with Carleton Industries and the discovery items that somehow ties into your job—otherwise you'd be blabbing."

Putting my head down, I again attempt to pass him, but he plants his legs like a football tackler preparing for a block. "Red," he says a little too gently, given how frustrated I know he must be. "There are at least two people dead, including your mother. Of all times, this isn't the time for you to go attorney–client privilege on me."

I agree in principle that this isn't the time for me to play by the rules or invoke the attorney–client privilege—if it even exists. The list is protected, but I doubt the privilege extends to watching a criminal act using my work product. When I weigh the scales, the living have to win. If I'm labeled a whistleblower, my career at Carleton Industries or anywhere else in the legal world will be over.

Maybe if I take a more aggressive approach, I can push one of Brian's buttons and distract him. "Have you found out who killed my mother yet? Or who broke into my car? It seems to me that you, as the real life detective, should be investigating instead of playing cat and mouse with me. After all, these open cases are getting colder by the minute and I don't see you having any suspects in custody."

My words are harsh, but I don't stop. "Do you realize that none of the women at Sunshine Village feels safe? Barbara Balfour may sing the Wahoo Police Department's praises and thank you for being her personal hero, but the residents don't share her opinion." I can't tell if Brian is listening to me or getting mad. He merely stands there.

Annoyed that he isn't trying to defend himself, I press on. "Last night, I had Shabbat dinner at Heidi Shapiro's and she and the Mah jongg group reached out to me. They want me to join with them to create an ad hoc investigative team because they think the police aren't capable of figuring things out before someone else gets hurt or killed. I told them that was silly, but now I'm not all that sure they aren't right about the police's capabilities."

I'm sure I've hit a nerve, but Brian still doesn't fight back. Instead, he moves away from my car and says, "Guess nothing's changed from the good old days." He walks away. I refuse to call out or follow him.

I get into my car and lock it, but I don't start the engine. I'm shaking too much—maybe from my anger at Brian for simply walking away or from my choosing to hurt him rather than admit what I know was an unlawful corporate activity. In my frustration, I slam my hand against the steering wheel, accidentally hitting the horn. The blare pulls me up short. I rest my head on the wheel, once again losing control of a flood of tears.

I've cried more in a week than in most of my lifetime.

Pulling myself together, I raise my head and vow to shed no more tears. If my mother leaving me taught me one lesson, it's that tears don't change reality. The Maj group is partly right—if I'm going to find out who killed my mother and hurt Carolyn and whether the same person caused Lindy's death, I have to look beyond Brian and Officer Robinson. I may not know much beyond the fact that my mother and Lindy are dead and that someone vandalized my car to steal the letter my mother gave me, but for any hope of getting answers, I have to take matters into my own hands.

Chapter Twenty-Five

Sunday morning and I feel almost normal today. A week has passed since someone killed my mother and I'm no closer to knowing who that person is, but nevertheless I feel like me again. Up at six, I take a quick jog and promise myself that I will get back into my regular exercise routine. After a quick shower, I go to Sunshine Village to attend the early Sunday morning service with my father followed by having brunch with him and a much-recovered Carolyn Holt.

I chuckle when we go in for brunch. Somehow, since she returned from the hospital, Carolyn has gotten herself assigned to sharing a table with only my father in the dining room. An aide squeezes a chair in for me to join them for brunch, but it is obvious, as I shift my body to the side so that a place setting can be added, that three is a crowd at this table. I'm not sure how Carolyn pulled it off, but my father and she seem to be enjoying the new arrangement.

Still, looking around the room at all of the other tables set for four or six people, my curiosity gets the best of me and I have to ask, "How did you manage to get them to set up a table for just the two of you? I thought part of the dining experience includes group interaction?"

Carolyn reaches out so her fingers brush against my arm. "Oh, Barbara and I had a discussion about the fact that there comes a time when being interrupted while one eats or simply the effort of carrying on long conversations is frustrating. Barbara agreed with me that as much as your father and I are people persons, it would be better for us to get used to quiet meal times now." She leans toward me. "You understand, don't you?"

And I do. Once again, Carolyn is making the way easier for my father. I bend forward before she can straighten up and give her a quick kiss. When I thank her for being so caring, she brushes me off. "Carrie, if I didn't get involved with activities and the lives of the people here, I'd go crazy or shrivel up and die. I made the decision when I moved here that this is my home and your father, you and everyone here are my family."

I frown. I understand what Carolyn is saying, but while it is helpful for my father now, in the long run I'm afraid she may be hurt. Looking around the room, it seems to me that most people don't follow her philosophy. They seem to have their own little pockets of friends rather than being part of one large family.

Before we can continue our discussion, one of the residents, a man wearing green and yellow, plaid golf pants, walks up to the little platform at the front of the dining room and asks for everyone's attention. Once we quiet down, he announces that the Sunshine Village Fifth Annual Poker Tournament will be held in two weeks.

When he sits down, I ask Carolyn if there is a Mah jongg tournament, too. "No," she says, "we don't have enough players yet."

I know the "yet" means one of her next activities will be arranging a Maj class. I hope she finds enough prospective players so I don't get roped in as an extra body to round out the count.

Our pleasant brunch goes way too fast. I kiss my father and Carolyn good-bye and then I feel I have no choice but to be on my way to my usual Sunday afternoon locale—my office.

CHAPTER TWENTY-SIX

One part of me wants to skip going to work today. Although last weekend was Indian summer, with people cramming in one final barbecue or day of swimming or boating on the river, I was glad to spend my time in the office enjoying its air-conditioning. This weekend is different.

The cooler temperatures have spurred the leaves to a medley of oranges, reds, and yellows. I'm tempted to walk or bike along the Riverwalk to take advantage of the crisp weather. Instead, I enter my office building, show my identification badge to the guard on duty, and sign the weekend roster. Because my line of the sign-in sheet is only number seven, I know very few fools like me are working today.

The quiet proves beneficial. I quickly draft a memo on a complex tax question respecting a proposed 469-D reorganization that CI hopes to do in Ireland. I'm proofing the memo when I realize I am not alone. Lester Balfour stands in my doorway.

"Did you enjoy your dinner last night?" he asks.

"Yes, sir. Did you?" I've seen him in the building before, but never on my floor and definitely not in my office.

"I'm still trying to unclog my veins," he says. I try to figure out how he knew I was here today and if this has anything to do with my last CI assignment or my choice of companions last night. "May I sit down?"

He is seated in my lone guest chair before I can do more

than nod. "I saw your name on the sign-in sheet." He examines my office, taking in my diploma and the pen sketches hanging on my walls of Wahoo's Bridge and the Riverwalk. "To be honest, I debated whether to come and speak with you, but last night, after Barbara told me about your father's condition, I felt I should."

That Barbara and he talked about my father raises my antenna even higher. Surely, like the attorney–client privilege, Barbara, as Sunshine Village's executive director, has a legal obligation under HIPAA or some other law to protect the privacy of the retirement home's residents. I can't help but wonder what else they discussed about my father and me.

From the tone of Balfour's voice, I'm uncertain if I should read his presence as friend or foe. Stranger things have happened in business, but I'm more inclined to be wary. "You probably don't know this," he says, "but my wife died a few years ago after a fairly quick bout with early-onset Alzheimer's."

"I had no idea, sir. Neither Barbara nor anyone else ever mentioned it."

"Barbara's mother died shortly before she began working at Sunshine Village, so I guess it never came up." He fixes his steel-blue eyes on me. "She tells me your father has the same gentleness of spirit and frustration with the disease her mother had." I am too astounded to respond.

"After we ran into you last night, Barbara also told me how much she admires your ability to juggle things with work and being there for your father, especially as he is starting to decline. I admire those qualities in a child. Barbara was like that with her mother."

He doesn't look at me directly as he drums his fingers on my desk. "You know, we have a generous policy for using family leave to be with a sick parent or child. Have you thought about using some family leave to take your father on a nice vacation while you still can?"

"I always thought there had to be a medically documented illness to use family leave. My dad has dementia, but he's nowhere near terminal. I'm saving that leave," I hasten to add, "in case I need it later."

"But later, he won't know if you're there or not. You need to take a few weeks off with him now." I'm beginning to smell a rat. Lester Balfour may be acting caring and kind, but the man I met in Fourth's office is the type of businessman who frowns on being sick for one day, let alone out on maternity or family leave. "Believe me," he continues, "I've been there."

He pauses for too long a moment as he tries to gauge my reaction. "If it is a matter of economics, Barbara and I have a condo about four hours from here that we would be glad to let you use for a couple of weeks."

Even as I wonder whether the condo is in Orange Beach or San Destin, I know not to accept his offer. "Thank you, but I couldn't do that . . ."

"Nonsense. We rarely use our Orange Beach place and definitely have no plans to be down there for the next couple of weeks."

"My work?"

"Not a problem. Take a laptop or, better yet, for a couple of weeks, we can reassign some of your tasks. Most of the work will still be here when you get back, but time with your father won't." His tone and manner as he insists on making this out-of-the-blue offer is relaxed, but directly contrasts with the intensity in his eyes.

"Mr. Balfour, I truly appreciate your kind offer, but I can't accept it."

He glares at me.

"You barely know me, and although your daughter knows my father, both of you are being far too generous to us." I speak quickly, hoping to prevent him from getting a response in. "Besides, as you well know, this past week has been a difficult time for us personally. I think it best that my father stays in the environment in which he is comfortable." I don't add that I'm afraid breaking the chain to my desk probably would translate to coming back to no job.

He sits erect, resting a manicured hand on my desk. Not only is he no longer drumming his fingers, but he has misplaced his smile. "You realize there is a limit to not only the time he'll be able to travel, but also to the time he can be a resident at Sunshine Village? Both may be quite short."

"I realize all of that, sir." I hold up the pad on which I've been drafting the reorganization letter. "But, I think it is equally as important for me to fulfill my responsibilities to Carleton Industries as to my father."

"Ms. Martin, feel free to think about my offer for a day or two." He stands and starts to leave. I find myself marveling at how his perfectly creased pants have no wrinkles, but I clearly understand the meaning of his words. "I hope you do fully understand your obligation to Carleton Industries."

Although Balfour is merely stating the obvious, I shiver as he leaves. Then I pull my cell phone from my pocket.

CHAPTER TWENTY-SEVEN

Instead of being at dinner, my newly enlisted investigative team waits for me in the four white rockers that flank the patio outside the back door of Sunshine Village. From the patio, one has a good view of the Japanese garden. As instructed, I approach the Japanese garden and the patio from the Riverwalk. I wave at them. They are right. I can go it alone and get nowhere or join forces with them to figure out which hand the tiles make.

All of this could be part of a bad movie, but that's because of the sour taste Lester Balfour's visit left in my mouth. Had he not come to see me and pressure me, I'd probably still be loyal, goody-two-shoes Carrie. Hopefully, I can sidestep implicating myself to the police or the company. The greater likelihood is that, like Michael, I may be job-hunting when all this shakes out. In that case I won't have severance pay; but, as my father has often told me, the most important thing a person can have, my integrity, will be intact.

When I phoned Heidi a few hours ago to say I was ready to go renegade against the Wahoo police force, she reminded me that, as the Mah jongg group suggested during our Shabbat dinner, we would be most effective if this was a "covert operation" for now. We weighed the pros and cons of our "mission" and I left it in her hands to arrange this meeting. That's why I'm back at Sunshine Village during dinner hour, while my car is parked at CI.

At Heidi's instruction, I walk quickly through the first

122

entryway, the Japanese garden entrance. The garden is in bloom with flowers of all varieties and colors lining either side of the pathway to the building. The evening is warm. A breeze gently rustles the leaves on the trees.

Now that I'm closer to the four rocking women, I see all are gray-haired, with perhaps a tinge of Sunshine's reddish rinse. Pink-coiffed Heidi is missing. I scan the faces of the women and realize Carolyn is in the fourth rocker.

"Heidi is waiting for us in her apartment," my favorite librarian tells me. I must appear perplexed by her presence because Ella quickly volunteers that Carolyn is the Maj group's new permanent fifth, so it seems only right to include her as part of our investigative team.

"Without Lindy," Carolyn cracks, "I won the spot by default." No one objects to her comment about the deceased.

All at once, the four, almost in unison, rock forward as a means of helping themselves stand. Watching this maneuver, I think of how my cadet mates at the academy would prep as a group for our 5-mile run. I vow to get back to the gym and keep my core muscles strong forever. At the same time, I have second thoughts about whether my gray- and pink-haired team members are physically and mentally fit for the job ahead of us.

"Come on," Ella commands. "Heidi wants us to get you upstairs before too many people see you." She pokes her head through the rear door and peers to her left and right before waving me forward.

"Stay close to the window side until you get to the back stairwell," she whispers loudly. "Marta and Barbara are sitting at the first table in the dining room, but they can't see the window side of the patio from their table." She peeks again. "Okay," she instructs us, "to play it safe, give Hannah and me a moment to walk through the dining room and keep them busy."

Without waiting for our response, she grabs Hannah's arm

and pulls her to the dining room, chattering about something nonsensical. Once they are inside the dining room, Karen, Carolyn, and I follow Ella's directive of sticking to the window wall until we reach the stairs. My earlier impression of their endurance was wrong. Age has not diminished the vitality of either Karen or Carolyn, as both take the steps to the sixth floor without being winded.

Despite our good clip and their having played decoys in the dining room, Ella and Hannah wait for us at Heidi's door. Each scours a different side of the hall. When Ella, chief lookout, sees us, she knocks twice on Heidi's door, pauses, and gives the door two more quick raps. Heidi flings the door open to let us in, but slams it behind me so quickly she almost nips my heels.

The six of us huddle in her entranceway until the sound of a male throat being cleared catches my attention. Michael sits in a folding chair by Heidi's card table, which again is ready for a Mah jongg game. My team already has betrayed me. Although they are unaware of how guilty I feel about my tangential role in Michael losing his job, I am frustrated they invited him without asking me. Feeling uncomfortable at the idea of working with him, I begin to leave, but Ella and Carolyn block the door.

"Sit down, Carrie," Heidi orders.

"Please." Michael gestures to the couch where his mother and Hannah sat the first time I visited this apartment. Ignoring his outstretched hand, I choose one of the tufted wing chairs. The others assort themselves among the seats, except Carolyn, who remains by the door. I wait for Heidi to explain Michael's presence, but Karen speaks for the group.

"We know that when you called Heidi, you were asking us to work with you as we discussed Friday night, but we talked it over," she pauses letting me take in the reinforcing nods her friends give me, "and we feel Michael has value to add to our endeavor." Michael looks uncomfortable. I am curious if Karen has a business degree in her past. Maybe, she simply watches a lot of stock and money shows.

I choose my words carefully. "I know you all respect Michael's legal abilities after the way he helped Hannah last year, but his inclusion wasn't part of our deal. Perhaps you would do better working with him than with me." I think I've just uttered the perfect line for my exit, but Carolyn disagrees.

"That's enough grandstanding, Carrie." She moves to the side of my chair. "We have a job to do. Acting like a spoiled child won't figure out who did this to me."

She turns her bruised left cheek, so I can see it clearly. Considering Carolyn knows how upset I am at losing my mother and her being beaten, showing me her cheek to make me stay seems like a cheap shot. Of course, it works. I hardly listen to the rest of what she is saying. "Leaving won't help us find out if the deaths of Lindy and your mother are related or the result of an unfortunate coincidence."

"Or how the documents I marked disappeared in the night," Michael adds.

Carolyn had me convinced to stay, but Michael's comment hits too close to home. Again I get up to leave. Carolyn's icy stare freezes me to the tufted upholstery.

"Carrie, if you were the police," Heidi asks, "how would you have handled this investigation?"

"Definitely not like Babyface," slips out before I censor myself. "I would be more like Brian, getting everyone to tell me their stories." I've started, so I continue, "Letting people talk freely is better than asking a lot of questions." I don't mention that it also is a good time to sit back and observe how people respond. Some talk too much, some too assuredly, and some claim to know so little that it is obvious they are lying.

"Then, for each of us to decide what is relevant, I think we need to start at the beginning, without editing any details this time around," Heidi declares. "Michael, please take notes for us."

She opens a small drawer in the table next to the couch and takes out a pad and a pen, which she hands to Michael. The cuckoo clock in her apartment chimes six times. When all is quiet again, Heidi turns to Carolyn. "What do you remember about last Sunday?"

Carolyn leans on the back of my chair. "Last Sunday," she begins slowly, "was the usual confusion leading up to the Halloween Children's Fair. I hung the banner, then went to make sure the games were ready in the card room: tub and apples for bobbing, go fish in the giant pumpkin booth, and pin the hat on the witch. They were, so I went back to my room to get into my Burberry costume for the carnival."

"About what time was that?" I interrupt.

"Probably about twelve thirty or one o'clock is when I put on my boots, raincoat, and hat."

"Did you have anything on under your raincoat?" Michael asks.

"Michael!"

He rolls his eyes at his mother in the same way Molly does when I say something she doesn't agree with, but he waits for Carolyn to answer.

She gives Michael her library frown. "Of course. I put the raincoat over the jeans and blouse I already had on." She resumes her story. "Once I had my costume on, I went down to the dining room to meet Hannah. We were setting up for my ghost-story hour when I realized I'd forgotten to bring my treat bag downstairs."

Carolyn turns to me. "You remember the candy and children's books I used to give out during my story hour at the library?"

I nod. I always left the Wahoo Library's Halloween story hour with a new book and my favorite candy bar.

"Well, I do the same thing here."

Only now, I think, she undoubtedly pays for the candy and books herself from her pension, no longer salaried by the beneficent Lindy Carleton. I make a mental note to make a contribution or shop with Carolyn next year.

"Anyway, I remember walking into my room to get the bag of treats I left on top of my dresser, but I can't recall anything after that. I must have been hit right when I entered my room because I don't even remember everything going black. Everything else from that day is pretty blurry."

"What about seeing my mother? Was she in your room on the day she was killed?"

"I never saw her, Carrie. I've been told she was found wearing my hat and coat, but I don't know how she got those things from me unless she took them after she hit me."

Michael looks up from the notes he is taking. "What makes you think she was the one who hit you?"

"How else would she have gotten my clothing?" She raises both hands palm up and shrugs. "It doesn't make sense to me. The Charlotte Martin I knew years ago would never have done something like this." She stops and stares at me. "But, I never thought she would leave Peter or you, either."

Chapter Twenty-Eight

The silence in the room is broken when Michael bumps his leg against the card table, causing the neatly stacked tile walls to collapse. He starts to rebuild them from the tiles now lying loosely in the center of the table, but stops when his mother orders, "Leave them alone. Molly set the game up for us. When she builds the walls, she puts all the jokers so I get them in my first two picks."

"We didn't realize the first time she did it," Hannah volunteers. "We thought the good Lord finally had seen fit to help Heidi with her game."

For a moment I fear the game will need a new regular. Heidi sits so erect it is apparent Hannah has hit a nerve. I surmise Heidi may not be the best player, but apparently no one is allowed to comment on whether she wins from skill or luck. With a flick of her pinkish hair, she regains her investigative composure and steers the conversation back to the day my mother was killed. "What do you remember, Hannah?"

"Carolyn pretty much told you everything."

"Humor us." My assuring Hannah that her version is important is self-serving. I need to observe her demeanor. "You never know what detail you unconsciously picked up."

Ella gets up and grabs a glass from Heidi's drain board. She fills it with water from the sink and walks back to her seat, muttering, "I thought it was dull when Jess had us helping to trace everyone's genealogy, but this police work stuff is much more boring."

I try not to laugh as I assure her she is right. "It's a lot of repetitive interviews and paperwork. So, Hannah? What about you?"

"Where should I begin?" None of us answer. She glances at Heidi and Karen before she hesitantly speaks again. "Well, you know, I was making sure the room was ready with the chairs arranged in a horseshoe."

Michael stops writing and leans forward. His lips move as if he is about to ask another question, but instead he simply stares at her.

Hannah locks eyes with him. For a moment, she reminds me of a schoolteacher explaining a concept for the fifth time to a kid who just can't grasp it. "That way," she explains to all of us, "parents have a place to sit during the hour that their children sit on the floor right in front of Carolyn." She waits, seeing if Michael has any questions about the physical layout. I'm sure he has seen this parent–child seating plan used at numerous meetings involving Molly. When he relaxes back into his seat, Hannah picks up the thread of her story.

"Like Carolyn said, she came in all buttoned up in her Burberry raincoat and accessories to help me set up the story area. We were arranging the last chairs when Carolyn realized she didn't have her treat bag, so I told her to get it while I finished up. When she didn't come back in a reasonable amount of time, I went to her room to get her before more children arrived."

"Why didn't you just wait for her?"

"Because it was so out of character for Carolyn to be late. She always is fifteen minutes early. I guess I was afraid something bad had happened."

"And it had," Michael says.

"Yes," Hannah agrees. I am afraid from the manner that she

curls her lip that she is going to cry again at the memory of finding my mother, but instead she stands up and faces me. Putting her hands on her hips, she says, "Everyone here already knows the rest of my story from when you questioned me the night we found her. But, what were the two of you doing?"

Michael and I exchange looks and he picks up the story. "I was on my way to Mr. Martin's room to get Molly when I saw all the commotion on the floor."

"Were you on the floor when they called the Code Blue?" I ask.

"No," he answers. "By the time I got there, people were milling around the hall and Barbara was standing near the nursing station, trying to disperse them. Barbara told me Carolyn was dead and the police were in the room. I sized up the situation and told Marta to take Mrs. Schwartz to Mom's apartment while I helped Barbara get the onlookers back to dinner, watching TV, or simply going to their rooms. Once we got rid of almost everyone, Barbara and I were leaning on the nurse's station when we heard moans coming from the linen closet. I thought the linen closet would be kept locked, but . . ."

"To protect the linens from us," Ella notes.

". . . while Barbara was fumbling for her master key, I tried the knob. The door opened and . . ."

"You found me pulling a Lady Godiva in Burberry boots."

"Yes, that's right."

From Michael's slight grin, I think even though the rest of the day was horrible, the memory of this moment still tickles him, but he is too much of a gentleman to admit it.

"The next thing I remember," he says, "is Officer Robinson bending down next to Carolyn and noticing you, Carrie, on the other side of the nurse's station."

All eyes turn to me. "I followed Babyface, er, Officer Robinson, from Carolyn's room. Before that," I explain, "I responded to hearing the Code Blue for Room 346 being paged when I stepped off the elevator because I recognized the room number as Carolyn's. I immediately went to see if she was okay. There was a crowd gathered outside her room, but Ella was guarding the door. I worked my way to the front of the crowd and, Ella, you let me slip in."

I stop for breath and look at Ella. She smiles at me.

"Once I was in the room, I'm sure I glanced at Marta and Hannah standing just beyond the body but . . ."

"You didn't know it was your mother at that point?" Karen asks.

"No," I say closing my eyes to replay the scene in my head. "Actually, my eyes went right to the knife and Burberry coat, then to Marta and Hannah. I bent to check if I could help the woman I believed was Carolyn, but Marta shook her head to let me know it was too late to help."

"Had Marta touched the body?" Heidi asks, looking at Hannah.

"I'm not sure, but I think she did. The only thing I remember clearly is standing there screaming until Marta held me. She must have turned me so I couldn't see the body or the door. Carrie, I don't remember you coming in and even though I know you told Marta to take me out of there, I can't picture your face mouthing the words."

"That's right. You were turned away with Marta's arm around you when I suggested you leave," I acknowledge. "After the two of you went into the hallway, I started to follow you out of the room knowing good police procedure is to perfectly preserve the crime site, but I didn't leave because I felt Carolyn shouldn't be alone."

"How sweet of you to care about me that much, Carrie."

I feel my face getting warm. "Once Marta and Hannah left, I looked around." I don't mention that I locked the door or used

131

my mother's envelope to avoid leaving any fingerprints. Reverting to my police training when someone I care about is dead might sound harsh to these family-oriented women. "I sensed something was out of place or was staring me in the face so hard I should see it, but I couldn't figure out what felt strange. At a loss, I tried to preserve the site for later. I got on my knees to say good-bye to you and I picked up the edge of your hat to see your face one more time before the police came. It was at that moment I realized I was looking at my mother."

Even now the memory upsets me. As I blink to hold back the tears I promised not to shed anymore, Carolyn steps behind my chair again and rests her hands on my shoulders.

"I'm so sorry you have to go over this again." She gives my shoulders a gentle squeeze. I wonder if she can feel the involuntary way I shudder. "Carrie, what else can you see in your memory's eye?"

I shut my eyes and try to visualize the room. "Only jeans, boots, and the stuff from the candy bag strewn across the floor. But I clearly hear Babyface banging on the door and ordering me to open it, which I did."

Michael stops writing. "I don't recall seeing you in the hall until I'd already found Carolyn."

"That's because Babyface and I were in Room 346 going 'round and 'round about my overstepping my bounds by being *in* the room with the body with the door shut. As he sarcastically pointed out, he didn't know I was a 'detective.' "

"It sounds like he had a point," Karen observes.

"He did, but I couldn't stand to let him know he was right. I may not have finished the police academy's program, but I bet I remember more about what's right procedurally than Babyface ever knew."

Michael begins to say something, but I don't hear what it is because Hannah asks me a question at the same time. "Why did you drop out of the academy?"

"Because I realized it wasn't right for me. I liked the investigative part, but to be a good cop, you need that special touch with people, like my father has." I tighten my grip on the arms of my chair as I mutter, "I guess I got my mother's genes."

Carolyn squeezes my shoulders again as Heidi asks, "So, what do we make of all this and does any of it fit in with Lindy's death?"

"I can't see any obvious connection between the two deaths," Carolyn says, straightening up. "To me, it feels like coincidental timing. It was dark. How do we know she didn't stumble and fall at that point on the path? Or, maybe she had a stroke?"

"Lindy didn't fall." Karen walks across the room to face Carolyn. Effectively caught between the two of them, I sink lower in my chair. "Of all of us, Lindy knew the Riverwalk like the back of her hand. She was so involved with it from its inception and through her daily walks that you could have put Lindy out there blindfolded and she wouldn't miss a step."

"But if she did have a stroke," Carolyn volleys back, "all her knowledge of the Riverwalk wouldn't have kept her from losing her balance."

Point to Karen. Counterpoint to Carolyn. I'm about to say something about how Lindy's cane lay on the rocks far above where she was found with her head bashed in from behind, but the cuckoo bird's insistent marking of the hour overrides my words. We've been brainstorming for a full hour, but I'm not sure we're any closer to a solution.

Michael says, "Carrie, I hate to run, but I've got to get Molly."

"Where is she?"

"With your father." Michael stumbles on his words. "Um . . . We ran into him in the lobby after my plans for her fell through, and I was coming up here to tell Mom I wouldn't be able to stay. Carrie, your father amazes me at how well he still reads people. He asked me what was going on and before I knew it, I found myself telling him everything, including that Mom wanted me here for your brainstorming session but my babysitter flaked out."

I can't believe the irony of it. If not for my father's ability—despite his dementia—to do what he always excelled at, Michael wouldn't have been here. As Michael continues telling me how my father graciously invited Molly for dinner and a reading session afterwards, I glance at Heidi. Though I can't read her mind, I'm sure she can read mine, and know exactly how much I think Michael is incapable of keeping a secret.

"Continue talking," Carolyn says. "I'll go downstairs and take Molly off Peter's hands." She is out the door before she can possibly hear Michael and Heidi thanking her.

I start to follow her, but Ella makes a comment that stops me in my tracks. "Your father and Carolyn are related, you know."

"Excuse me?"

"Jess did our charts and found ways that we're all tied together. Hannah and I have direct ties to George Washington."

When Hannah nods yes, I don't even try to hide how perplexed I am. "George Washington?"

"Not really," Heidi says, again opening the drawer in the table next to her. She sorts through some papers in it and pulls out two sheets. "When Jess first got into genealogy, she used a computer program to generate our family trees. By accident, she did the first few with a sample program that filled George Washington's name into one of the boxes to demonstrate how the program would populate."

Heidi hands me the first sheet so that I can read it. Sure enough, a line ties Heidi Shapiro to George Washington. "She ran the entire Mah jongg group at the same time, so the error was on all of our charts. Even though she gave each of us a corrected genealogy chart, we all kept the original one so we could tease her about how she could have considered, even for a moment, four Jewish ladies having ties to a Revolutionary War figure, especially since Washington never had children of his own."

Michael explains, defending his deceased wife, "It was one of those things where you work with something so long, the error doesn't jump out at you."

I'm well aware of the truth of that. It's why I always wait a day, if possible, before proofreading important documents I draft. I know what something I write is supposed to say so when I review it too soon, my eye skims over the little errors.

Thinking about missing obvious things, I realize that even though I saw nothing unusual when I reviewed the pictures on my phone the other night, it probably would be a good idea for me to check them again. Maybe something I heard tonight will help me see something different in the photos. Needing to digest what I have heard and wanting to go over the pictures again, I suggest we end our brainstorming session for today.

To my surprise, Heidi agrees. "Perhaps," she says, "if we sleep on what we've been discussing, one of us will wake conscious of something we overlooked."

The way everyone nods, I guess the Maj group puts a lot of stock in dreams.

CHAPTER TWENTY-NINE

As Michael and I walk down the stairs to my father's third-floor room, chatting about nothing, his cell phone rings. "Sorry," he says, pulling it from his pocket and checking its caller ID. He quickly pushes the answer button and tells the caller, "Just a minute."

To me, he mouths, "I've been waiting for this." He turns his back to me and walks back up the stairs, talking quietly into his phone. Although he isn't facing me and he speaks too softly for me to overhear, his body language shows intensity I have not yet seen him display. By the time I make up my mind to go on without him, he calls my name. He is off the phone and with long strides catches up to me in the stairwell.

"Sorry for being so rude, but I've been waiting for that call for a few days."

"No problem."

"Well, I have a problem. I have to go out and I can't take Molly. Would you mind walking her back to my mother's place and asking Mom to put her down for the night? I'm afraid I'll be tied up for a while and Molly has school tomorrow."

The moment I acquiesce, he starts running down the stairs to the first floor. I call after him from the third-floor landing, "What should I tell Molly?"

"That I love her and I'll be here in time to take Nana and her to breakfast before school," Michael calls over his shoulder to me. Then, I hear him stop on the stairs and he yells up at me

136

to "wink at her after the breakfast part—she'll laugh 'cause she knows my mother isn't capable of having her makeup on in time for school, much less breakfast." With that he is gone, so I continue to my father's room alone.

Apparently, the third floor is the place to be tonight. Not only can I hear laughter coming from my father's open doorway, but I see that the nurse's station is being staffed by Marta—and Brian? What's he doing here again? The two of them are so deep in conversation that when I say, "Hello," Marta actually jumps. For a moment she is so flustered that she introduces me to Detective McPhillips. Brian reminds her that we've met before. She blushes, obviously remembering Brian and I "meeting" when Carolyn was injured and my mother's death was discovered.

To help her save face, I ask, even though I know the answer from the laughter I hear, if Molly is still with my father.

"Oh, yes," Marta answers. "Both Ms. Holt and Molly are in there with your father. Molly was reading to him for the last hour or so—until Ms. Holt got here. Since then, the only thing coming out of that room has been the sound of them cutting up."

We are still talking in this stilted way when the elevator door opens. Barbara Balfour makes a beeline for the nurse's station. She seems a little surprised to see us there, but smoothly shifts her attention to Brian. I can't help but notice that this time, when she moves close to him, Brian doesn't react in quite the same manner he did when she flattered him during the impromptu party in Carolyn's room. "What are you three talking about?"

"The laughter coming from my father's room. Listen." The four of us are quiet enough that we hear my father "mooing."

"That's one of the better animal imitations that Mr. Martin and Ms. Holt have been making," Marta tells her.

"Did you check to make sure they were okay?"

"I did about forty-five minutes ago, Ms. Balfour. They are playing a game. When a player lands on a space with an animal, the player picks a card and has to make the sound of the animal before moving forward on the board. Each time one of them does an animal noise, they all go into gales of laughter. I didn't want to ruin their party by interrupting them again."

"Well," I say, pointing to my father's room, "I certainly hope my arrival isn't a party downer."

CHAPTER THIRTY

"Hello!" Though I speak more loudly than usual, I'm not sure the three of them hear me over all their laughter at my father, who is holding a card in his hand and "mooing." I join them. My father makes a fairly sick sounding cow.

We stop laughing when Molly, peering beyond me, asks, "Where's my daddy? Is he okay?" The fear in her voice is clear.

"Your daddy is fine," I assure her. "We finished our meeting, but he had to go see someone." Both my father and Carolyn give me inquisitive looks behind Molly's back, but I ignore them. "He's going to be late and you have school tomorrow so he told me to take you back to your Nana's for tonight and assure you he'll be here bright and early before school to take Nana and you out for breakfast."

Although Molly's lip curls into a pout when I tell her she is spending the night at her Nana's, her reaction to my wink following the line about taking Nana out for breakfast produces exactly the reaction Michael predicted. "I gather your Nana isn't much of a morning person?"

"Nana doesn't take her eyeshades off before ten." Ah, the honesty of a child.

"But I thought everyone has to flip the green/red sign on their door by nine or they get a phone call from the front desk."

"Not Heidi," Carolyn says. "They don't check her door before eleven."

"Nana forgot about the sign one morning, shortly after she

moved in. She was so asleep, she didn't hear the phone ringing in the other room or them knocking at her door."

"Ambien," Carolyn volunteers.

Molly gives Carolyn a "Molly" look for interrupting her story. "Anyway, the person checking on Nana called Ms. Balfour, who came upstairs to unlock Nana's door. She had a key, but Nana had put her chain on, too. The maintenance people had to break the chain to get in before Ms. Balfour could walk into Nana's bedroom. When she got to the end of Nana's bed, Nana rolled over, pulled her night eyeshade up, and told Ms. Balfour to 'leave me alone, and fix the chain on your way out.' Then Nana went back to sleep."

I can see Heidi doing that—eyeshade, pink lacquered hair, and all.

"From then on," my father says, "they've had each person in independent living fill out a card telling the hour they want to be checked on. I think they were afraid Heidi would have her lawyer son come after them."

"Lindy would have pursued a complaint through a hired hack, but not Heidi," Carolyn observes, helping Molly put the game pieces back in their box. Watching them, I notice that, like me, both are left-handed.

Afraid our conversation will deteriorate into pure gossip, I tell Molly to get her stuff together. She gives both my father and Carolyn a good-night hug before picking up her little pocketbook and a stack of books from my father's nightstand. "We read all of these." She holds them so I can count six spines. Most of the titles are from the *Amelia Bedelia* series. Knowing my father, he found the books charming and the reader even more so. I know I do.

We head to the elevator. Brian stands alone at the nursing station. "What happened to Marta?" I ask.

"Barbara had something she needed Marta to help her with

downstairs."

"They left the nurse's station unattended?"

"I guess they did."

"That's weird. Barbara is a stickler for protocol." Brian raises his eyebrows at me. "The home's requirement is that there always is at least one nurse or aide on the floor. At this hour, Marta would have been manning the floor alone so it seems weird Barbara took her off the floor."

Just then the elevator door opens. An aide gets out and walks behind the nurse's station. "I guess that answers that question. By the way, were Marta and you talking about anything in particular when I got here before?"

"Not really." Brian comes around the nurse's station. I notice his tie is in his coat pocket and his collar unbuttoned. "Carrie, can we get a drink tonight? I feel badly about how we ended Saturday evening, plus there are some things I'd like to run by you."

He projects that little-boy look I've always found hard to resist. More important, after my meeting with the Mah jongg group, some gaps in my reasoning surfaced. I think he can fill them in so I won't have to wait for a dream to make the connections. "After I drop Molly off at Heidi's, we can go for a drink or talk here, whichever. I have only one caveat."

"What's that?"

"If we go for a drink, I want to take my own car."

"No problem. I'll meet you in the lobby."

CHAPTER THIRTY-ONE

Apparently, in Michael's haste to get away, he took a moment and called his mother, because Heidi is waiting for us. I leave Molly with Heidi and then go back to my father's room to kiss him good night before meeting Brian in the lobby.

"Let's get out of here," Brian says. Then, like the old days, he adds, "I'm tired, Red. Do you mind driving and bringing me back later to get my car?"

No problem for me. I have the keys to leave if he annoys me. I hope he has cab fare.

As I turn on my headlights and back out, the car facing mine is illuminated. So are the two people sitting in the front seat. Startled, they duck their heads, but it is too late. In the moment they were spotlighted, it was easy to see their faces.

I continue backing out. "That looked like Michael," Brian says. "Do you know the woman he's with?"

"It was Michael. And yes, I know the woman," I answer, stopping for the red light at the intersection. "Jaimie Carleton."

"Related to the Carletons?"

"The Fourth's daughter. Lindy's only grandchild."

CHAPTER THIRTY-TWO

Brian lets out a low whistle as I whip into an easy parking space at The Pub, Wahoo's version of an upscale bar, which offers a limited but excellent food menu. Except for my recent medicinal use of wine, I'm not much of a drinker, but I do love my food.

It's almost nine p.m. on a Sunday night, but The Pub is hopping. Soon we're settled in a rear booth, with Brian beating me to the seat that puts his back to the wall. Some parts of police training are never shed. We order a beer for him and a glass of wine and order of spinach-artichoke dip for me.

"So," Brian asks, "what do you make of what we just saw?"

"I'm not sure. I don't know much about Jaimie Carleton except that after she graduated college she was sent abroad to work at one of the family subsidiaries. She's been back about six months, but other than saying hello in the halls, I haven't had any contact with her."

"What do you think Michael's connection to her is?"

"Again, I don't know. He said nothing about her when the three of us talked at the FattBurger, and he never mentioned her tonight."

"During the secret brainstorming session?" Brian grins at what I know is a quick rising of color on my face. "Red, there are no secrets at Sunshine Village. A lot of innuendo and misinformation, but information about covert investigative teams meeting has a way of getting out."

I sip my wine to gain time while trying to decide how much

Brian is bluffing me versus how much he actually knows. Unlike the Mah jongg ladies, I always trusted Brian. Now, after seeing Michael with Jaimie, I'm weighing who my best ally will be in finding out what happened to my mother. Before I make a strategic commitment, I decide to make him show his hand.

"Secret investigative team? Tell me more."

"Aw, come on, Red. Molly told me she had to stay with your father because Michael, her grandmother, the other Mah jongg players, and you were having a secret meeting to solve the crimes that the police haven't been able to figure out."

Who says eight-year-olds don't have big ears? No filters, but definitely big ears.

"We were only brainstorming a little."

"Carrie, I know you better than that." Brian's eyes connect with mine and, even though I want to look away, I don't. My body language has to make him trust me if I'm to get the information I need.

"Caught, sort of," I admit.

"Sort of?" He leans back against the leather of the booth and sips his beer. I counter by popping a chip covered with spinach and artichoke dip into my mouth. Two can play the delay game. "Carrie, I've been working as hard as I can to discover who killed your mother and Lindy Carleton."

My antenna pops up. I swallow quickly. "So, you do think both were murdered? By the same person?"

He nods. "Possibly. I keep trying to make sense out of what I thought Lindy said when I found her on the rocks. You know she was hit hard from behind and then sustained injuries falling, so none of us can tell if she was consciously making sounds or not. Sometimes I think she was simply moaning in pain; but, other times I think she was trying to tell me something."

"What?"

He shrugs and takes another swig.

About Lindy, at least, that quickly makes my mind up. Brian and I need to pool our thoughts. "Shut your eyes."

He complies.

"Think back to when we were on the path."

He doesn't speak, but from the way he purses his lips and keeps his eyes closed, I know he is concentrating. "Good. Tell me what you see and hear."

"I hear a whimpering sound that I know isn't a cat. It's the sound of a person. I've heard it before." He doesn't elaborate.

"That's why you recognized the screech? Because you've heard it before?"

"Yes, in Dover." He frowns, but keeps his eyes closed. I don't press him. Instead, I gently guide him back to the minutes with Lindy.

"I'm listening, trying to pinpoint where the person making the sound must be, but everything is dark and quiet again until you shout, 'Brian, here.' I'm a few steps beyond you, so I turn around to see what you are calling my attention to. Even when I get closer to you, I don't notice the cane at first. I only see the cane's tip when you point to it lying below the path."

"I know what I think I remember, Brian, but tell me, how do you see the cane positioned?" I sit quietly, waiting to learn if our memories are the same.

He opens his eyes and looks at me. "Red, the cane was lying perpendicular to the path and water, rather than parallel to it." I let him process his thoughts. "So, Lindy probably was facing the water rather than walking the path when she fell."

"That's how I see it, too. She used the cane in her right hand, so if she had stumbled while walking, she would have fallen on her side and the cane would have either fallen with her or landed parallel to the path. I think she had to be facing the water."

"Because the cane was lying perpendicular to the path?"

"And also because of the way the cane's rubber tip faced

toward the path." I grab the fork lying on my napkin and stand up to illustrate my point. Oblivious to the diners occupying the nearby tables, I step forward pretending to slip. I raise my right arm during my pratfall so I flip the head of my imaginary cane backwards. The released fork follows my arc. It lands with what would be the rubber side out in the same way we saw the cane, but at more of an angle. "See what I mean?"

Brian doesn't move as I rise from the floor, but one of the waitresses runs to help me. She shoots him a dirty look as she steadies me and asks, "Are you all right?"

"I'm fine. I slipped, but I caught myself. Not graceful, but no damage done. Thank you."

I slide back into the booth, deliberately not making eye contact with any of the other patrons I'm sure are staring at me. With the waitress glaring at him, Brian starts to ask me if I am all right, but stops mid-sentence having a coughing fit. He covers his mouth with his napkin as he coughs again, preventing the waitress from seeing him choking on his own laughter.

"I'm fine, really," I assure the waitress, who leaves after giving Brian an even more ominous glare. When the waitress is out of earshot, I ask Brian what direction Lindy was lying in when he got down to her.

"Angled, from having rolled, with her head more to the right if you face the water from the Riverwalk."

"That's what I thought from the way the paramedics brought her up on the stretcher. They used ropes and a pulley system, so I figured that other than slipping a backboard under her, they wouldn't have turned her. She had to have been facing the water."

"But, wait a minute," Brian says. "Are you sure that if she stepped off from walking in either direction, the tip of the cane wouldn't have faced the path anyway?"

I think for a moment, and then shake my head. "Remember,

when we learned about gravity and kinetic energy in junior high?" I don't wait for Brian to answer before I sing him the little ditty we were taught to remember the difference between the two types of energy. "Based on Lindy being in motion, there isn't another logical explanation."

"Nice demonstration," he admits. "Not perfect, but I think you made your point."

"You agree with it?"

"Absolutely." Brian softens his tone while raising his voice. "Are you sure you're okay?" He puts his hand on mine. I think I'm sitting with Dr. Jekyll in his Mr. Hyde mode until I turn and look over my shoulder. The waitress is nearing our table with a man who I suspect is the manager.

"Absolutely fine," I say to Brian, covering his hand with my other one and speaking loudly enough so everyone can hear. Acting surprised at the presence of the Pub's representatives, I repeat my assurances to them and thank them for their concern. The manager tells us our tab is on the house and gives me his card if my slacks need dry cleaning.

Once we're alone again, I slip my hands from his and rest them in my lap while Brian resumes talking.

"I don't know the why, but I definitely agree with you that Lindy was pushed. At one point, I thought Lindy might have been trying to say 'pushed,' but what I actually heard was 'pu,' and later, when she seemed to rally a bit, 'pu' again. Unlike Officer Robinson, who from the moment we brought the body up has been convinced Lindy was murdered, I didn't feel right putting too much stock into what I thought I heard. I wanted to wait until we had confirmation that her head injury couldn't have been caused by her fall."

"For once," I interject, "I agree with him."

Brian continues his train of thought. "Chief Johnson wants both of these investigations done by the book—one step at a time. I agree with him but remember, Robinson is responsible for the Carleton case and he is gung ho to solve it."

"And you're not gung ho to find my mother's killer?"

Brian doesn't respond. Without thinking, I snap a chip against the table. Even though my mother was barely back in my life and I may have taken her as a bag lady when she first stood in my doorway, her death deserves to be investigated with the same energy and intensity that is being accorded to Lindy Carleton.

Brian's silent stare unnerves me. He is the detective on my mother's case, but I wonder if he, too, is more interested in finding Lindy's killer. Maybe it's an ego thing? Normal protocol would call for a detective to be responsible for both cases, but apparently Chief Johnson is either giving Officer Robinson a chance or buying into Babyface's argument that Brian's presence and involvement at the site required assigning the case to someone else in the department.

I challenge Brian by making a crack that I'd be skeptical about any conclusions Babyface forms, but I am interrupted by the trill of my cell phone. I don't recognize the number, but I opt to answer it. Before I even finish my hello, a woman's voice, which I recognize midsentence as Ella's, screams into my ear, "We need you. Babyface arrested Marta!"

"What?"

"Heidi is trying to get hold of Michael, but she asked me to call you. Babyface thinks Marta killed Lindy Carleton."

"I'll be right there."

Brian gives me a quizzical look. This time the concern on his face is genuine.

"That was Ella. Officer Gung-Ho just arrested Marta for Lindy's murder. Come on."

CHAPTER THIRTY-THREE

We go straight to Heidi's apartment. The Mah jongg group, together with a wide-awake Molly, is waiting for me. I'm not sure how to read their reaction when Brian comes in, too. When Ella sits across the apartment at the Mah jongg table and Karen doesn't offer either of us a piece of cake, I fear it's not especially positive.

"Detective McPhillips," Heidi begins, but Brian cuts her off.

"Carrie and I figured out Lindy was pushed."

Karen inserts herself into the conversation. "Officer Babyface seems to have come to that conclusion faster than the two of you." I don't get a warm and loving feeling from the glare she gives me.

"But," I ask, "why arrest Marta?"

"He's convinced she's the only one who doesn't have a good alibi for last Monday evening."

"Excuse me?"

"Most of us were welcoming Carolyn home."

"True, but Marta was changing my father's sheets. I was with her before I came to the party in Carolyn's room."

"But," Heidi points out, "there was a gap between when we all left Carolyn's room and when any of us saw Marta again." I realize she is right. I also note, as Heidi mentions Carolyn, that Carolyn isn't here.

"Where is Carolyn now?"

"She went with Michael to help put up a bond. Even though

this is Sunday, Michael hopes to bail her out."

"Judge Holley makes all bail decisions," Hannah volunteers. "He had my case last year. We were a little strident . . ."

Karen cuts her off. "We were downright defiant."

I can imagine what a "little strident" translates to. The story I heard being told about Hannah's arrest and the Mah jongg group's reaction included a lot of name calling and shouting.

"You know," Hannah interrupts, "we've been here so late, my cat needs to be fed. Molly, come with me." Molly's expression shows the last thing she'd like to do is feed Hannah's cat. She wrinkles her nose and frowns. Slowly, she turns her head toward her grandmother who locks eyes with her. I can't blame Molly. The conversation is getting interesting.

After they go, Heidi explains to me, "My son thought Marta might fare better if Carolyn went with him. She wasn't involved in Hannah's case last year and the judge knows her from when his children used the library."

Observing the earnest faces before me, I have to agree with Michael's judgment on this one.

"The really bad thing," Ella offers, turning the loose tiles lying between the racks face down, "is that today is Sunday." She moves the tiles around in a way that's similar to shuffling cards. Finally happy with how she mixed the tiles, she begins building the walls. "Michael is afraid Judge Holley won't do anything about bail until tomorrow."

I realize that Michael and Carolyn must have gone to the judge's home trying to get him to take action tonight.

"What about a jail bond?" I look at Brian when I pose this question.

He shakes his head. "I guarantee Robinson will paint this case as such a sinister murder, there won't be a jail bond. No one will want to touch this case with the proverbial ten-foot pole."

No one except Michael, I think.

"When was she arrested? Brian and I saw her when I went to fetch Molly from my father's room."

Once again, the Maj women give me suspicious looks. Brian picks up on their mood. "Let me clarify that," he says. "I was talking to Marta at the third floor nurse's station when Carrie came off the elevator. The three of us visited until Barbara came onto the floor and told Marta she needed her downstairs."

I note how he carefully leaves out our plans for getting a drink or the time gap where Marta and he were alone again when I went into my father's room.

"Did Barbara say why she needed her?" Heidi asks.

"No, and as Carrie pointed out to me at the time, it was against Sunshine Village practice for Barbara to leave the nurse's station and third floor unstaffed." I nod. "We were questioning the unmanned desk when an aide arrived to cover the floor, so we didn't give it another thought."

Karen puts down the cake knife she has held since we walked into the apartment. "Did you two leave the building together?"

"Yes. We went to get a drink away from Sunshine Village to discuss the murders."

I know I don't have to justify being with Brian, but as hurt and betrayed as I felt when they included Michael without telling me, I don't want them to think I've given up on our investigative group. "I thought Brian might have some information that could help us sort things out."

One of the Maj group, Ella, I think, combines a snort and a "Really" that makes me wonder if the Maj girls are more concerned with the murders or my going out with Brian instead of Michael.

Karen turns the cake around as if looking for a flaw in its icing and then presses further. "You two must have passed them arresting Marta."

"It seems like we should have," I agree, "but we didn't know anything about her arrest until Ella phoned me." I change the subject. "How long ago did Michael leave?"

"You just missed him. I got him on his cell phone about the same time Ella caught you. He picked Carolyn up and immediately went to try to help Marta," Heidi says.

"So what do we do now?" Although I pose the question rhetorically to the entire group, I look to Brian for an answer. I think about the beef Lindy and Marta had over the hanging of the pants but can't believe anyone, even Babyface, would think that enough of a motive for Marta or anyone to commit murder.

"I think I better get down to the station," Brian says, "and see if I can learn what broke in the case that led to Marta's arrest."

I start to say I'll go with him, but he shakes his head. "Red, you may think like a police officer, but to us on the force you're a lawyer. No one at the station will cross that boundary. I'll get more information alone. Wait here until Michael or I call."

As Brian heads out the door, Ella, pausing from her tile-wall building asks, "Carrie, you've met Judge Holley, haven't you?"

"Yes."

"Well, maybe you could simply call him and explain this silly misunderstanding? I hate the idea of Marta being locked in a cell with criminals."

Although I cringe at the idea of Marta in a jail cell, too, I shake my head. "I don't think that would work. My calling him would probably end us both up in a cell."

They say a good lawyer knows the law while a better lawyer knows the judge. I've been CI's briefcase carrier to a few motion dockets, and from those limited appearances I know Judge Holley is a snake.

I didn't always believe that. When I first came back to Wahoo he was running for re-election, so he came to speak to the

Women's Guild of our church. We all found his bowtie with mini-judicial scales and his presentation delightful. Now that I've encountered him in the courthouse, I realize he was kinder and gentler while on the re-election circuit, knowing if he got beat he wouldn't qualify for the nice pension that awaits him.

"Calling won't work with Judge Holley. We'll just have to wait to see how persuasive Michael and Carolyn are." I'm not sure why Michael took Carolyn with him from a legal standpoint, but perhaps he feels her previous involvement with the judge's children might open up a chink in his usual demeanor.

Heidi joins Ella at the card table. She sits across from her. "While we're waiting," Heidi says, "I think it's time you learn how to play Mah jongg."

CHAPTER THIRTY-FOUR

I look around Heidi's apartment until I understand Heidi is talking to me. "With Carolyn and Hannah not here, we need a fourth to play."

"But I thought you need five people?"

"No, only four," Karen explains, taking one of the remaining two seats at the table. "Traditionally, the game was played by four men, but the Americanized version that developed in the 1930s calls for five people. The rules were standardized by The National Mah Jongg League in 1937."

"When Sadie Moscowitz played with us," Ella says, "we were hoping to book one of their league-sponsored cruise tournaments, but she moved away before we could arrange it. Maybe, with Carolyn, we'll be able to take the next cruise."

"Perhaps." Karen looks straight at Ella. "One of the good things about Mah jongg, according to some studies they've been doing lately, is that it has been shown to have a positive effect on the cognitive functioning of persons with dementia."

As Heidi points me toward the last chair at the table, it crosses my mind that I should ask Karen if she's ever thought about appearing on a game show. She'd be a natural.

Heidi begins flipping over some of the tiles Ella so carefully built into walls. "Do you know anything about Mah jongg?"

"Only that it's played with tiles. We played card games." I don't mention that "we" refers to not only my father, who taught me casino and gin rummy, but also to my friends, with whom I always played poker in the choir loft. Thinking about that makes me suggest, "Maybe with as much trouble as you've had keeping players, you should have played poker? The card room always seems full."

All three take their hands off the tiles, and stare at me, saying nothing, with the same expression of "Are you an idiot?" on their faces. Eventually, Heidi orders, "Let's get back to Mah jongg."

Karen takes over giving me my lesson. "There are a hundred and fifty-two tiles divided into nine suits. There are three main suits—craks, bams, and dots—each with tiles numbered like cards are, one through nine." She turns over a few tiles and pushes samples of each in front of me.

"I see. That's why I've always heard about things like 3 bams or 5 craks."

"That's right," Karen says. She taps on different tiles as she explains, "The appearance of the dots and bams are logical—dots and bamboo sticks. The craks resemble Chinese hieroglyphics."

I nod. So far, I'm okay with this game.

"The next suit is the winds, and these are marked with an N, E, W, or S for North, East, West, or South. They often show up in hands with the dragons, which are red, green, or white."

Karen puts three dragons in front of me. She tells me the dragon with the same red coloring as the craks goes with them while the green one matches the green bams and the white one is played with the dots. I pick up a white dragon. The only thing on the tile is a pencil-thin, rectangular, blue outline. "The shape of this reminds me of a bar of soap, not a dot."

"It must have reminded a lot of people of soap because the nickname for the white dragon is 'soap.' " Karen sets aside a few tiles that are pictures and tells me they are flowers and I don't have to worry about their numbers as they are considered all the same, as are the eight jokers. "Jokers are wonderful substitutes for everything except in hands that call for pairs."

Heidi starts rebuilding the wall Karen and she destroyed, showing me the different tiles. "The best way to teach you to play, now that you know the tiles, is to just do it. You can use Hannah's card. Your ultimate goal is to make a hand from your tiles that exactly matches one of the hands on your card."

She hands me a tri-fold card that has directions on the back and, inside, rows of tiny numbers or letters printed in red, blue, or green. There must be at least fifty rows covering the three sections. Karen points at her card, which she has laid on the table in front of her. "To keep the game fresh, the League issues a new card every year with that year's approved possible hand combinations."

"How do you keep from playing hands from last year's card?"

"You don't, always," Karen says.

"Sometimes, especially in the beginning of the year, you can sneak in an old hand and get away with it," Ella says, chuckling to herself.

Heidi frowns. "Don't try it, Carrie. The sequences may seem similar, but we all learn the new card and recognize its variations."

For a moment, I have a flashback to my mother lying on Carolyn's floor. Like the hands, there was an apparent variation—her sneakers, but it didn't register with me. After so many years, I took Carolyn's storytelling outfit for granted much as I bet some of the Maj players do when the new card comes out.

"See that 'x'?" Heidi asks, tapping a hot pink nail against my card. "If the hand calls for three or four of something, like three 5 bams, and the hand shown on the card has an x at the end of it, you can call when someone else discards a 5 bam to complete the last tile in that grouping."

"But," Karen explains, "other than the discard, you have to

already have the other tiles in your hand and then you have to expose the group of tiles called by putting all of them up on your rack." She lays a few tiles on top of her rack so I get the idea of what exposed tiles means.

Heidi ignores her. She points to the little "c" after some of the hands on the card. "That 'c' means a hand is closed and you can't call. If your tile to finish a series is thrown out, you have to adapt—that is, change what hand you were planning to play—because you'll never be able to make it come in to win."

I take a moment to glance at my watch. Surely Michael has pled his case for Marta's bail to the judge by now. I have to assume not hearing from Michael or Brian is a sign Marta doesn't have a winning hand. I only hope Michael has more than one hand that Marta's tiles can be converted to tonight.

"Let's play already!" Ella demands. "She'll pick up the game better if we just play."

Karen, who they say is East, picks four tiles for her hand from the wall in front of her and then pushes her wall of tiles into the center of the table where we can all reach them. Heidi takes four tiles and then Ella does the same. They wait for me to pick. We take turns picking four tiles at a time until we each have twelve tiles. Seeing the other women lean their tiles on the colorful rack in front of them so that only each can see her tiles, I do the same.

Because Karen is East and will have to discard first, she takes the first and third tile remaining on the wall while the rest of us, in order, only take one tile to give us a count of thirteen. We then do some passing—right, left, across and left, right, across— which the women say are "charlestons."

Finally, Karen, as East, throws a tile from her hand face-up onto the table to begin playing. Because I sit to her left, they look at me to pick a tile and decide whether to keep or discard it. As we play I barely recognize the names of the tiles let alone know what hand on the card the tiles I pick will most likely fit, but somehow I manage.

Although I have to concentrate on playing the game, I realize I also need to find out what Michael's relationship with Jaimie Carleton is while he isn't here. "You know," I begin, "in the last six months, I've been seeing Jaimie Carleton around the office. They say she'd been in Europe. Did she come to visit her grandmother at Sunshine Village?"

"Jaimie is a dear," Heidi answers, watching Karen, who nods her head in agreement and puts out a 4 crak. I wonder if Heidi needs the 4 crak but doesn't have enough of those tiles to call yet. Oy, I'm thinking like a real player! "She probably visited Lindy as much as you visit your father."

"That's funny. I never ran into her here."

"Because you usually came at opposite times. You visit your father after work while Jaimie started visiting her grandmother first thing in the morning while Lindy was in the rehab wing. Jaimie maintained her schedule of visiting before work when her grandmother moved into a minimal-assistance unit. As part of her self-imposed rehab, Lindy walked the Riverwalk morning and night, and Jaimie joined her in the morning. It's your turn, dear."

Interested in what she is saying, I pick a tile and quickly discard it, not even thinking if it might help my hand. "Most of us at work haven't had an opportunity to get to know her yet. The word is she went to Europe to use it as a finishing school."

Ella snorts. "Sounds like someone is telling stories about her like they told about Lindy."

"What do you mean?"

"Lindy was prouder of her granddaughter than she was of her son. Jaimie graduated Phi Beta Kappa from the University of Pennsylvania's Wharton School of Business, and then got an MBA from Harvard. Her grandmother made sure she was assigned to the overseas subsidiaries so she would have a better sense of the company's international dealings. Lindy always said her husband believed their international operations were where the future growth of the company would come from so she wanted Jaimie to understand how they worked."

"But I've heard her father plans to sell CI."

"He'll be hard pressed to do so, Carrie, without a bitter fight," Heidi says. She calls a tile and exposes three nine dots on her rack.

"While neither Lindy nor her son, and that would now be Jaimie and her father, individually owns a controlling interest, together they own the majority of the stock." Once again, from the straightforward way Karen presents her knowledge of the inner workings of Carleton Industries, I wonder if she has a business degree, plays the market, or has some kind of insider knowledge of the company.

"Lindy, may she rest in peace," Karen continues, "had several loyal backers in her corner, as does Carleton. Before her death, Lindy was working hard to make sure her backers and even some of her son's were aware of Jaimie's skills. Mah jongg." Karen flips her tiles onto the top of her rack so we can all see how beautifully her hand made.

"Very nice," Ella says. She starts turning the tiles on the table over to ready them for the shuffling process. As we begin building walls again, she explains to me, "We're not playing for money today, but if we were, that would have been a very nice hand." She points to the place on the card where there is an assigned value next to the hand. "Depending on whether you pick it or someone gives it to you, or whether the fifth, if she is playing, bets on you, you can make different multiples of that value."

I don't respond. She lost me at the value on the card, but something Heidi said triggers an idea in my mind.

"Mrs. Shapiro . . ."

"Heidi, dear."

"Heidi, Michael told me Lindy had a real interest in environmental issues. You mentioned that Lindy and Jaimie often walked together. Did she share that interest with Jaimie?"

"I'm sure she did, but I have no idea if Jaimie felt the same way. Michael does, though." She finishes building the wall in front of her and, as East, picks the first group of tiles. I am picking first when she says, "He and Lindy could talk about water and pollution for hours on end. But I don't ever remember Jaimie being part of those conversations."

We continue playing for a few minutes before I pose another question to the group. "Are Michael and Jaimie friends?" Again, I'm so focused on sleuthing that I throw a tile Ella calls. As she already called once and exposed four 6 dots, I should have realized the possibility of her needing the soap I threw away.

"They know each other, but, unless Michael was bringing Molly to me, he usually, like you, already was working when Jaimie came to visit Lindy."

My game playing and interrogation is cut short by the return of Michael and Carolyn. She drops into the closest chair while Michael walks over to us. Although he still has his coat on, his tie pokes out of where he stuffed it into his pocket. "Judge Holley set the bail hearing for tomorrow at nine."

"Oy gevalt!" someone cries.

"Marta has to stay in that horrible cell with all the weekend drunks and other hardened criminals?"

"No, Ella," Michael says. "Brian interceded with Chief Johnson so Marta can be in a cell by herself."

"What about a jail bond?" I ask.

Michael shakes his head. He shrugs out of his jacket and collapses into the other overstuffed chair. "Apparently, before she was arrested, Babyface made a big play to the prosecutor about Marta being a flight risk and a murderess in a series of crimes."

160

"Not Marta," Heidi objects.

"We know that, Mom," he says, "but this case got assigned to a new prosecutor who, rather than looking into the facts, argued everything he was spoon-fed. We'll get it straightened out in the morning, Mom."

"How is she?" Karen demands.

"Very grateful to have loyal friends like you. Where's Molly?"

"She's with Hannah. Why don't you still let her stay with me tonight like we had planned? I'm sure you've got some things to get ready for tomorrow."

"I do, but I hate to impose." He gets up and gives his mother a kiss.

"She's my granddaughter. You're not imposing. Go get her. Molly already thought she was spending the night with me, so when she knows you're helping Marta, she'll have no problem letting me be the one to take her to school."

None of us say anything, but I'm sure we're all thinking about the fact that Heidi doesn't do mornings. Heidi is the one who breaks the silence. "Who do you think got up every morning to get Michael to school on time?"

"Thanks, Mom." He kisses her again.

"Now, hurry and get her. I need to put us to bed before it's time to get up."

I realize what a sacrifice Heidi is making for Marta. Under other circumstances, I'm sure that, if she keeps Molly, she insists, as Michael had planned on doing, that he pick Molly up early enough to take her to breakfast and school.

"Carolyn," he says, "if it still is okay, I'll meet you in the lobby around seven thirty tomorrow morning to give us time to be ready for when Marta's case is called."

CHAPTER THIRTY-FIVE

I am in the courtroom early to get a good seat. I hope that when Marta's case is called, she sees me sitting here and knows that, even though she may not have any blood relatives in Wahoo, she has plenty of extended Sunshine Village relations. As I wait for Judge Holley to enter and the docket to begin, Brian comes in and takes a seat on the other side of the courtroom. Although our eyes meet, he does not acknowledge me. Under today's circumstances, I think that is wise.

We all rise when Judge Holley enters the courtroom. He tells us to be seated. Marta's case isn't called until almost ten a.m. My impression that Judge Holley is not a jovial jurist continues to be reinforced. He never cracks a smile. It is a good thing I have vacation leave because he also moves slowly. In fact, everything involving Judge Holley and the Wahoo court system takes an extra-long amount of time.

When Marta's turn comes and she stands before Judge Holley, I see how frightened she is. As small as Wahoo seems to me, for a real country girl like Marta, Wahoo's jail is one big-city experience I'm sure she never expected to have—nor deserves. Michael does an excellent job of arguing or else the prosecuting attorney is no longer as adamantly opposed to Marta's freedom as Babyface, because bail is quickly set.

I slip out of the courtroom and see Carolyn, Marta, and Michael huddled together. Although I don't know for sure, I bet they are discussing the next steps of making bail. I continue walking. From the corner of my eye, I observe Brian leave, too. He catches me in the hall and we exit the building with him a few steps behind me.

"Carrie," he whispers. "Don't turn around. Keep walking, but listen to me. The three of us need to talk. If you're willing, Michael and I will meet you at your apartment as soon as possible."

This cat-and-mouse side of Brian is so out of character that it scares me.

"Please?"

"Okay," I whisper, though I'm not sure anyone can hear me out here on the street.

"We'll get there as soon as we can," he says, peeling off in a different direction as if we had come to this point together by happenstance.

Because I am unsure of when they will arrive, I call in that I'm taking the rest of the day off. I need time to pick up the jeans I left on the floor last night, throw out the newspapers from the past week, and run the vacuum. I kick off my shoes, and, though it is not yet lunchtime, I pour myself a glass of wine for fortitude to straighten my apartment while I wait for the boys.

CHAPTER THIRTY-SIX

Michael and Brian arrive just after lunch. Truth be told, I am wary of having them together in my apartment. We sit around my well-used kitchen table, the same one Brian and I bought at a garage sale six years ago for our apartment. I offer wine, but both prefer water. As they exchange glances, I am the one who feels out of place.

"I think the time has come for the three of us to pool our information for Marta's sake," Brian says.

For once, I don't disagree with him. Even if he isn't officially assigned to Lindy Carleton's murder, I know that he is far more levelheaded than Babyface. I also realize that meeting like this could have negative consequences for all three of us.

"Michael," Brian continues, "tell Carrie what you told me about your discussion last night with Jaimie Carleton."

"First, you have to understand, I don't really know Jaimie Carleton other than to pass in the hallways at Sunshine Village. Lindy thought highly of her and was grooming her to eventually replace her son."

"I imagine that's not an idea that would sit well with Fourth."

"Or with Lester Balfour," Brian says.

"I'm sure it isn't," Michael agrees. "But, Lindy made certain that Jaimie is ready to assume a leadership role by ensuring she understands both the overseas and the domestic operations. When she brought Jaimie home from her last international posting, Lindy could honestly say that not only did Jaimie have book smarts, but she had, at some point in time, worked every type of Carleton Industries job from assembly to high finance. Somewhere along the line, Lindy also instilled into Jaimie a corporate sense of civic and environmental responsibility."

"Was she a part of the pro-bono lawsuit?" I ask.

"Not per se. Knowing what was coming down the pike, Lindy spent a good many walks over the past few months showing Jaimie where the spillage occurred and talking to her about its ramifications. Even though Jaimie was made aware of what was going on between Lindy and Jamie's father, Lindy deliberately tried to keep Jaimie out of that fight."

"So, Brian and I did see you with Jaimie last night, didn't we?"

'Yes."

"And she was the one who called on your phone. The one whose call you said you were waiting for?" Michael emits a wordless sound in agreement. "Why?"

"After the discovery fiasco that cost me my job, Carleton Industries demanded the lawsuit be withdrawn. With Lindy's death and other things being more pressing, the attorney handling the case for my old firm put drafting the dismissal paperwork on a back burner. I figured what could I lose? After her grandmother's funeral, I called Jaimie and asked her to meet with me. Last night, she finally returned my call. So much for our not being seen."

"Did anything come out of the rendezvous?"

"Only that Jaimie shares her grandmother's feelings about pollution, not her father's, but she's pragmatic. Unless there's evidence of continued polluting, she doesn't see a way to avoid dismissing the case. Lindy and Jaimie were looking for signs of continuing pollution during their walks, but they never saw anything overtly suspicious."

"Like more dead fish or detergent swirls?" I suggest.

"Right," Michael agrees. "And, they didn't have a way during their walks to test or compare the water with the results in CI's issued testing reports. Part of the discovery items that I swear I marked were testing results."

I push away from the table and go into my bedroom. From my hamper, I pull the jeans I wore the night Lindy was killed and fish through the pockets to find the sheet of paper Fourth missed shredding. Without a word, I toss the crumpled piece of paper on the table in front of Michael and Brian. Brian smoothes it out and they read it at the same time.

Michael lets out a low whistle. I peek at the paper, but, other than again seeing it has a few dated phosphate-reading levels signed by a technician, it has no meaning for me. "Where did you get this?" Michael asks.

"It was the night Lindy was killed, wasn't it, Red?"

I nod and then tell them what I saw that night. "Even though I didn't know what it was, I had to pick it up after I saw it fall behind the shredder. It didn't mean anything to me, so I put it in my pocket and forgot about it."

"If the date of these results can be confirmed, which I feel sure it can, this will be big for us!" Michael turns the piece of paper over to examine its blank back. "Given that I identified it as a document to be photocopied, this will go a long way toward proving CI knew it had excessive levels of pollution, *even* after the date they declared they were in compliance."

Michael doesn't have to spell it out because my law background tells me one piece of evidence won't be enough. If the technician can be found to attest to his signature and his testing, that changes things. It's a big "if"—locating him and hoping he hasn't been bought off.

Part of making this stick in a court of law, I also realize, is my having to testify to my role in the discovery and to what I witnessed as the cover-up using the list I made. Integrity versus job security looms before me like a neon sign.

Michael stands, still holding the paper. He runs his free hand through his hair and stares at me. Finally, he says, "Why did you wait so long to tell me about all of this? Didn't you realize this piece of paper might have helped me keep my job and credibility?"

I can't answer him and, for some silly reason, I struggle not to cry, this time. Michael simply keeps staring at me.

Brian takes the paper from Michael. He lays it down again on the table and turns toward Michael. "We may be able to put a little pressure on CI to resolve this without a lot of fanfare."

"How is that?" Selfishly, I'm thinking about my job and reputation. I'm going to need time to find another job in the future. If my part in this doesn't become public, I may have a paid opportunity to balance my father's care with finding a new job.

"Sunshine Village is a private retirement center."

"So?" I'm perplexed.

"Even private retirement homes have to be owned by someone, Red. You know from the Maj players and Lindy, in particular, there were a lot of rumblings about food quality and staff cutbacks. Once again, Lindy picked up the ball. She brought the complaints to Chief Johnson's attention and he promised to investigate them. When he assigned the task to me, he meant for it to be a courtesy, 'everything is fine' overview. You know me: I couldn't resist poking my nose in a little deeper than perhaps Baby—uh, Officer Robinson would."

"You found something?"

"I'll show you. Carrie, do you have your laptop?" Brian keeps talking as I bring my computer into the kitchen and power it up. "When I pulled the Certificate of Need related to the number of beds for Sunshine Village's medical facilities, I didn't recognize the corporate name listed as its holding company."

Debra H. Goldstein

The opening screens come upon my monitor. Brian tells me to pick a search engine and type in "Sunshine Village + Wahoo, Alabama + Certificate of Need." I follow his directions and we get a string of entries. "To save you the time I went through, click on that one." He points to an entry near the bottom of the screen.

I click on it and an article from about eight years ago comes up discussing that a certificate of need to move beds has been filed on behalf of Sunshine Village by its corporate parent, Retirement Industries, Inc. At the end of the article a corporate entity, LB, Inc., is mentioned as the filer.

"So?" Michael asks.

"Now, run a search on Retirement Industries, Inc."

I do as Brian instructs me and within a few seconds we find another article referencing a holding company, LB, Inc., that actually owns Retirement Industries, Inc. The result is an abstract of the Articles of Incorporation and other filing papers for LB, Inc. At the very bottom of those I find the agent for LB, Inc.—Lester Balfour.

"Mr. Balfour is LB's agent?"

"He *is* LB, Inc.," Brian says.

I click back to the holding company article. "Brian, you mean Lester Balfour is the majority owner of Sunshine Village?"

"That's how I interpret it. I couldn't find any evidence that he divested it as a holding."

"Does that tie Sunshine Village to CI?" Michael asks.

"No," Brian and I both answer simultaneously.

"Ditto," I say.

Michael glances from Brian to me. "It's from a child's game," I explain. "If two people say the same thing, you say 'ditto.'" Michael continues to have a funny expression on his face.

"Okay," I say, "that's not important. What *is* important is that Sunshine Village is not a property of CI. It either makes or loses

168

money directly for Lester Balfour. Based upon the data I see, it looks like he went into the business when it was making lots of money."

"So?" Michael asks as I type a few more things into the search engine. I open and close a few screens and then turn the computer so Michael and Brian can read what I've left open— two national pie charts plus a news article.

"I can't find any direct connection between Barbara's arrival and an earnings dip, but unless Sunshine Village was out of the norm, these reports all show there should have been such a loss."

Brian points to a difference in revenue from physical therapy between the two charts and asks me if that is what I'm referring to.

"It's one of the things. If you remember, after all the big health-related fraud cases, changes were made requiring Medicare payment documentation and there was greater scrutiny over how physical-therapy reimbursement is calculated. The result nationwide was a lower profitability line for the same provided services."

I lean back from my laptop. "I'm not saying Barbara has done anything wrong, but I bet, at a minimum, the complaints about food quality and staffing are true. No telling what kind of cuts she has made trying to stay profitable."

"There's a little more to it," Brian says. "Because Sunshine Village has a sister facility in Tennessee, we may be able to invoke the possibility of a crime occurring across state lines. At least, we've used it before to bring the big guns in for some forensic help. It isn't another HealthSouth or anything like that, but there's been some book-cooking. We were about to pull the trigger using Marta as one of our chief witnesses."

"Brian, how were you using a nurse in an accounting-fraud case? She was on my father's floor doing patient care rather than running the show."

"Marta did jobs as assigned," Brian says.

Thinking about it, I remember my talk with Marta in my father's room the night Lindy was killed. She told me she'd seen a lot of folks at all levels with sticky fingers. At the time, I didn't think about who or how she had seen anyone who didn't live on the third floor. I tend to think about Marta as assigned to the third floor nurse's station, but, in actuality, since the day I moved my father in, I've interacted with Marta.

She quietly functions as Barbara's second in command, running interference between patients and staff. If not for Marta's broader role, I wouldn't have had anything to do with her until my father changed rooms and Lindy wouldn't ever have had a chance to complain about her.

Now I know why Brian wanted me to run the computer search. He would never compromise an active case, but, under the circumstances, he felt Michael and I needed more information to get to the bottom of everything. This way, technically speaking, we found it for ourselves. The precise extent of the funny-money situation remains to be seen.

"Brian, the reason I asked the Mah jongg group to help me is that Lester Balfour, in a veiled way, threatened me."

"What?" Michael says. "Mother didn't tell me that."

"That's because I didn't tell her or anyone else until right now. When I called your mother to accept the idea of collaborating, I explained that I'd thought about what the women said during Shabbat dinner, and I'd come to believe they were right—we could do a better job of figuring out things if we worked together."

I've just insulted Brian, but, instead of getting mad, he leans over and takes my hand. I don't make any effort to shake it off as he asks, "What did Balfour do to threaten you?"

"It wasn't what he did. The day after we ran into Barbara

and him at FattBurger, he came into my office and told me how he had lost his wife to Alzheimer's. He kept relating it to what my father is going through, and strongly suggested I take a few weeks off to be with my dad.

"Mr. Balfour pointed out how fast dementia patients spiral downward. He urged me to take advantage of the quality time I could have with my father by taking a vacation now."

Michael turns to Brian. "You're the policeman, but, from a legal standpoint, I don't see anything threatening about what he said to Carrie. Do you?"

I break in, and Brian listens. "It wasn't what he said at that point. In fact, he even urged me to use his beach condo if it was a matter of money."

"That sounds pretty nice of him. Maybe he really was trying to be a good guy."

"I thought so, too, Michael, until our last exchange. It was his tone when I rejected his offer and put my work ahead of a vacation. His voice was like ice when he specifically reminded me he hoped I fully understood my obligation to Carleton Industries."

"What do you think he was referring to, Red?"

"For one thing, if I were to take a vacation, I might find on returning that my job no longer existed. It happens in big companies all the time. More important, though, there was and is no question in my mind his words had to do with Michael and the documents."

Michael scoffs, but before he can interrupt me I press on. "Michael, you were right. You weren't incompetent. I was simply too frightened for my own job and my future employability if I became known as a whistle-blower. When you confronted me at the FattBurger and again in your mother's apartment, I was too scared of how, if I lost my job, I'd be able to take care of myself and my father to admit what had gone down."

He picks up the piece of paper again and looks from it to me. I avoid his gaze by staring at a picture of my father pasted on the door of my refrigerator. Still holding the paper I retrieved, Michael walks away from the table. He runs his free hand through his hair and then comes back, but doesn't sit.

"Let me see if I understand this." He spreads his long fingers out over the wrinkled paper that he drops back on the table. "You got an assignment to follow me around. Right?" I nod affirmatively. "From?"

"Directly from Fourth. I was to follow the investigative team and write down the location and sticker number of whatever documents they showed interest in. Then I was to dutifully bring the list back to his office and hand it only to him. I complied with his instructions. He took the list from me and, without even glancing at it, he gave my list to Lester Balfour."

"Balfour?"

I nod. "Balfour was in Fourth's office when I arrived. Once Balfour understood my codes for each place, drawer, and sticker number, I was dismissed."

"And when you and I went back later that night?" Brian interjects. "When you ran back to me at the amphitheater, you had just seen them shredding documents. That's why you were so frightened."

I nod yes, almost out of breath from reliving the anxiety of that night. My stomach is in knots. "I was debating telling you when we heard the sound that was probably Lindy screaming as she fell." I look back at Michael. "Brian took off running with me behind him."

"But we were too late."

This time, I don't attempt to console Brian because something clicks for me and my mind is working in overdrive. "We were too late, but that tells us a few things."

It is Brian's turn to wait for my explanation.

"In hindsight, we know the scream had to be the moment Lindy was pushed so we're able to come up with a timeframe for the evening." I grab a pen and the lined pad near my kitchen phone and jot down an abbreviated list of that night's events.

Lindy screams

!

We run from CI to SV.

!

Pass no one

!

See L's cane

!

B. goes down the embankment

!

I run through the garden entrance to SV's back door (don't pass anyone)

!

Can't get in—door on night lock

!

Bang on doors and windows—shout

!

People come from dining room.

!

Barbara opens door, worried where I've been.

!

Karen B. tells me of my car alarm, broken window and Barbara calling the police.

!

Babyface arrives. What time?

That's all I write down, but I tell Brian and Michael what they already know—that the police and emergency crews responded to Barbara's second call for help, but it was too late for Lindy.

"We're talking about maybe a ten-minute time frame in which whoever pushed Lindy escaped. We know that person didn't come in Brian's or my direction on the Riverwalk and probably didn't go around the front, either, because Babyface was there. That would mean the murderer fled on the undeveloped part of the Riverwalk away from where we were or was able to get back into Sunshine Village from the back door."

"I doubt they went away from us along the river," Brian says. "Right now there isn't any lighting and the path is very narrow and uneven. Our people did check out that area, but they didn't find any evidence of footprints or anything that had been disrupted."

"Then it had to be someone with a way of getting back into Sunshine Village." For a minute I am stumped because even a resident couldn't have gotten in the back door once it was on lockdown. "Brian, there is one thing you haven't ever told us: what time did the first call that Babyface answered come in? How much time was there between the call about my car and the one about Lindy?"

"I looked at that."

"So, why haven't you mentioned it before? It could help us pin down the killer's whereabouts."

"I didn't mention it because the timing of the calls didn't really seem to have a bearing on anything. The first call came in just before nighttime lockdown."

"But it does help us. That means that if Robinson was in the front lot, someone could have had time to use the back door after pushing Lindy!"

I feel very satisfied with my deductive powers until Brian points out, "That brings us back to Marta, Barbara, and anyone who lives, works, or was visiting Sunshine Village during that period of time. Pretty much the same suspects we have for whoever broke into your car."

CHAPTER THIRTY-SEVEN

Night, with a multitude of dreams, comes, but restful sleep does not. I'm not sure whether pooling our information helped or hurt Marta. All three of us are convinced of her innocence—Michael who represents her; Brian, because he knows the value of the help she has been to his investigation of the financial shenanigans at Sunshine Village; and me, because I adore her. I realize adoration is a pretty lame reason to believe in someone's innocence, but at the moment it works for me. My biggest fear is if the retirement home is indeed in financial trouble, what does that mean for the patients? In Wahoo, Alabama, acceptable choices are extremely limited.

What if my father has to move in with me? This apartment was tight with Michael and Brian here for only a few hours. There's no question I would take him in, but how will I care for him when I'm at work, especially as his mind declines? The sharp edges of the kitchen counter, the open sockets, even the stove will need father-proofing—as one would do for a baby.

I force myself to stop thinking about the future. It only drives a larger hole into my heart. It is more important for me to concentrate on the past and the present. I reach for my cell phone to check the time and then remember the pictures I snapped right after realizing it was my mother rather than Carolyn lying on the floor. Perhaps I should have shared them with Michael and the Mah jongg group by now, but I selfishly wanted to look at them again alone.

Flipping through the few pictures I took, nothing in the room seems out of the ordinary except for the body lying on the floor amidst the candy. None of the shots shows my mother's face, but there is a clear shot of her sneakers and jeans sticking out from under the raincoat. That is the view that came into my mind when I was talking to Molly—when I realized I should have recognized her by her sneakers and jeans. Perhaps, in the first moment of seeing the body, I subconsciously put together the meaning of the sneakers versus seeing Burberry boots and that, rather than my feelings for Carolyn, is what made me turn back and lift the hat. Truth be told, I'll never know what tricks my mind played when I was alone in the room with my mother.

What I do understand is that I need to go back into the past with my father once again. Talking with the Mah jongg group on Sunday night and Brian and Michael yesterday led my subconscious to one dream in the few hours that I did fall asleep. A dream that opens a new area to explore with my one remaining parent.

CHAPTER THIRTY-EIGHT

When I get to Sunshine Village after work, my father is alone in his room. I close the door behind me, hoping anyone who might want to visit him will think he is sleeping rather than sitting, facing the garden, reading his Bible. I notice the Bible is the only book my father, always an avid reader, reads lately. I fear asking his doctor if this is a sign of further memory loss. The truth is, he's known the words of the Bible so well and for so long that he remembers all the stories and passages without a written text in front of him. I wonder if that's why he shows such patience listening to Molly read to him. Even if she reads the same book day in and day out, the stories are always new to him.

"Carrie, is something wrong?"

"Not at all. I'm standing here thinking how much I love you." I bend to kiss him and he pats my hair. One special characteristic of my father is he has always demonstrated his love for me, even at the times I was most exasperating.

I prop myself into a comfortable position on the window ledge so both of us can enjoy his view of the garden. "I see the flowers are blooming."

"Beautiful, aren't they? The days when flowers blossom and bees are cross-pollinating them for next year, are some of my favorite ones. But, you aren't here to listen to an old man's memories. Out with it, Carrie. You look ready to burst."

"I had a dream last night."

"Well, that's a beginning."

"I dreamed you and I were at a Vegas-type show watching beautiful girls with long legs, skimpy costumes, and big head-dresses."

"Glad to know I still like good entertainment," he quips.

"Yes." I chuckle at the image of him sitting at such a performance wearing his clerical collar, but, because that wasn't part of my dream I leave it out. "After the girls finished their number, their costumes morphed into normal clothing. Two of them came to our table: Lindy Carleton and Mother."

I watch his face for any reaction. It's slight, but there. "Did they know each other in Reno or is my dream making this up?"

"What does it matter?" He clenches his hands on the now-closed Bible resting on his lap. "What does it matter?" he repeats. "It was so long ago."

I kneel by his chair. "Dad, it's very important. It could be a matter of life and death."

"But they're both gone now."

"True, but Marta has been accused of murdering Lindy."

"Never." My father grabs my arm. "I need to help her. Marta is a good woman. You need to drive me to wherever she is." He struggles to rise, but I gently push him back into his chair.

"We can do her more good if you'll help me figure out who hurt Lindy and perhaps who killed my mother." He sits back, but I keep my hands lightly resting on his arms. "Please, Dad, tell me: did they know each other in Reno?"

"Yes." He sits and licks his dry lips. As he stares out the window, I am afraid for a moment that he might mentally pull away from me again, but then I realize he is collecting his thoughts to tell me the story correctly.

"For many reasons, not all of which I was privy to, your mother felt she had to leave us. She debated whether to take you with her, but she thought it would prove too confusing for you and might put you in an unsafe environment."

I want to ask how leaving me to grow up without her was the safe alternative, but hold my tongue to let him talk.

"You know Charlotte went to Reno." He pauses, lost for a moment in the past. "Your mother was a good-looking woman in those days. She had a lovely face with high cheekbones. I heard congregants say her looks were a cross between the serene beauty of Grace Kelly and the delicate charm of Audrey Hepburn. Her hair was more of an auburn shade of red than yours, which made her green eyes sparkle."

As I listen to his description of my mother, I understand why my father never married again. He never stopped being in love with her.

"She thought she would get a job as a waitress, but the first job she landed was a bit part in a chorus line—not exactly what a congregation would think best for a minister's wife, as she was to tell me later, but perfect for her at that point in time. The lead chorus girl took your mother under her wing. That was Lindy."

"So the story is true that Lindy didn't make it in New York but was a chorus girl when Carleton III met her?"

"Yes. Your mother and I introduced them, somewhat to the ultimate dismay of his parents."

"I'm confused. If Mom left you, how could the two of you introduce Lindy and Carleton III?"

My father leans back in his recliner. "Lindy was as beautiful as the garden out there. She was bright, quick, opinionated, and a good friend. She was also someone you wouldn't want as an enemy. Luckily, in just a few weeks, it was as if your mother and she were long lost sisters. They did everything together. Lindy is the one who taught your mother how to play nickel machines to get free food and drinks so her paycheck would go further. Lindy was the one who, even though your mother didn't want her to, called me after the accident." A look of pain crosses his face, perhaps remembering his witnessing her suffering as she recovered from the car hitting her.

"But how did Carleton III come into the picture?"

"I didn't have the money to go to Reno so I went to my friend and parishioner, Carleton III, to see if he would lend me the fare for the train. He did better than that. Carleton Industries owned a couple of planes for traveling between their holdings so he arranged for the two of us to fly to Reno. I was there when Charlotte woke up in the hospital." He smiles at the memory. "For the next few days, I held her undamaged hand each time she stirred."

"And Carleton and Lindy?"

"While I sat with Charlotte, she showed Carleton around. Lindy was only trying to be nice, but something clicked between the two of them."

"So they got married?"

"It was far from immediate. When your mother was getting back on her feet, Lindy insisted on taking her in. I arranged for them to have some help until your mother could manage, and I came back a few times—until your mother said seeing me was too hard. She wanted you and me to go on with our lives. I told her neither of us could go on, but she was adamant it had to be that way. So, I left her the letter to give you whenever she was ready."

"You wrote the letter? What was in it?"

My father ignores my questions as he continues with his memories. "I never saw your mother again until last week."

"What was so great a barrier we couldn't work it out to be a family? Didn't she love us enough to try?"

My father puts his hands on either side of my face and stares into my eyes. "Your mother loved you more than she loved herself. If you could have heard her singing and reading to you or watched how tender she was with you, you would understand. Somewhere, she got the ridiculous idea that by staying, she would destroy us. I couldn't convince her otherwise. You know how it is. There are times you are as stubborn as she was."

I don't know if I should laugh or cry. Part of me wants to protest that I can't comprehend her leaving us, but when it comes to stubbornness, I know exactly what my father is talking about. For years we fought about my behavior. I went from being the model little girl that was everyone's pet, like Molly is here at Sunshine Village, to rebelling against being in the fishbowl as the minister's daughter. My father gave me a lot of grief and took a certain amount of congregational flak about my cutting classes, staying out late, and doing other inappropriate things, but he always let me know he loved me.

To keep our conversation productive, I bring it back to Lindy. I ask how Carleton III and she kept up their relationship if my father never saw my mother again.

"During your mother's recovery, Carleton often flew to Reno to see Lindy and check on your mother. Once Charlotte was back on her feet and the divorce that she still insisted on was granted, your mother left Reno in the middle of the night. She didn't want to be a burden on any of us."

I don't interrupt my father, but I can't help thinking that my mother certainly had a pattern of leaving people who cared about her. Apparently, it never crossed her mind what a terrible burden it is to feel deserted.

"She did a good job of hiding herself because Carleton, Lindy, and I all searched for her, but with no luck. Eventually, I came home because I had both you and a congregation to tend to."

"And Lindy?"

"Carleton brought her home to meet his parents. And that, my dear, is an entirely different story for another day. Let's just say his parents may not have been delighted to have me perform the wedding service, but they were relieved it was a traditional wedding at the Oakwood Church and that, over time, they grew to love her very much."

The Lindy Carleton my father describes and the Lindy Carleton I met in Heidi's living room seem like two different people, so I ask him about the apparent change in personality.

"Disappointment can make one bitter, Carrie. Maybe Carleton and she had too strong a love or maybe their son is simply a weak man, but, after the death of my old friend, the relationship between Lindy and her son deteriorated. It isn't normal in either life or business to spar with your own child, and their relationship pained her enormously. But, she felt she couldn't roll over and let him do some of the things he was being encouraged to do."

"By Lester Balfour."

"By Balfour and others who don't care about people as much as they care about the bottom line."

"But Lindy had enough money, so why did she keep fighting her son?"

"For Jaimie's sake. That girl is Lindy's heritage to the world."

I want to ask more, especially about the letter my father wrote and who could possibly want to steal it now, but the privacy of the closed door is breached.

"Peter," Carolyn asks, "are you ready for dinner?"

CHAPTER THIRTY-NINE

I beg off joining my two favorite people for dinner. As I walk through the parking lot to my car, I run into Michael and Molly. My first thought is that Michael is bringing Molly to spend another night at Sunshine Village, and then I see that, like me, they are heading to their car. Sticking out from Molly's light jacket is a pink tutu. Knowing she carries her tiny, pink, patent-leather purse because it holds her epinephrine pen, I feel sad that it isn't because she's a carefree little girl who loves playing dress-up.

When she sees me, she lets go of her father's hand and does a modified pirouette for me. "Ballet day," Michael says. "It takes her hours to calm down after class, but, boy, when she finally goes to sleep, she's out like a light."

Silently, I envy her ability to sleep through the night as I say, "I remember being like that when I took ballet. I couldn't wait to show my father all my new moves. Looking back, I see he was very patient with me."

Molly grabs my hand. "Dance with me?"

"Oh, no," I groan. "My body isn't what it used to be."

"I'm not so sure about that," Michael says with a smile, catching me off guard. Surely, I heard him wrong. He didn't just make a pass at me in front of his daughter. I steal a glance to see if he is ogling me, but his eyes are on his dancing daughter. Obviously, I misunderstood him.

While Molly continues twirling and leaping, I lower my voice and ask him if he talked to Marta.

"Yes, I have. We're working on getting her back to work."

I'm surprised.

"Even if they don't let her come back until this is resolved, she needs a paycheck. Better to push to have her back on staff so she doesn't go insane at home." He claps his hands, and I join in as I realize Molly has finished dancing.

"That was wonderful. You're very good," I compliment her, because I mean it. For an eight-year-old, she truly is beautifully coordinated. Perhaps it's the time she spends with adults, or perhaps it's her nature, but she is far too wise for her years. Before I think of what I'm about to say, I blurt out: "You know, Michael, we should do something fun with Molly."

"Can we, Daddy?" Molly uses her eyes like a sad puppy dog, imploring him to do her bidding. If she is like this at eight, he doesn't stand a chance when she is sixteen.

"Not tonight." His eyes send a message to me for help.

"Oh, no, I didn't mean tonight. It's a school night."

Molly curls her lip in a pout.

To rescue Michael and distract Molly, I say the first thing that comes into my mind. "I have to work tomorrow, too. I was thinking more of having lunch at Suzannah's on Saturday."

Molly is absolutely placated, while Michael shakes his head. "Suzannah's?"

I smile sweetly as we walk toward his car. Suzannah's is a combination ice cream parlor, pizzeria, ride, and amusement park all mixed into one restaurant. Not only is a kid guaranteed a sugar high, but by the time parents buy extra tokens, their pocketbook takes a hit, too. Kids love going there. Michael unlocks his van and Molly climbs in. "Saturday it is," he says to me while Molly buckles her seat belt.

It takes all I can muster not to laugh at the way he pulls his mouth down and wipes a faux tear from his eye as he repeats seriously, "Until Saturday.

"By the way," Michael says, slamming Molly's door shut and leaning over the top near the driver's door, "Marta wanted me to tell you that when she picked up the sheets the other evening from your father's room, a copy of *Goodnight Moon* somehow got wrapped in them. The laundry sent it back with your father's laundry bag and Marta put it on the lower shelf at the nursing station. She didn't get a chance to tell you before Barbara took her downstairs to Barbara's apartment."

"So that's how it played out." I wondered why Brian and I didn't see Babyface when we were in the lobby or the parking lot.

"Right. Barbara told me Officer Robinson and she felt using her apartment for the arrest would avoid upsetting the residents by making sure any hysterics took place out of their view."

"How thoughtful."

"Makes me think more and more it was a setup."

"That thought crossed my mind, too," I say, thinking, like father, like daughter.

CHAPTER FORTY

When I get home, I nuke a slice of leftover pizza for dinner. I should have gone to the gym, but, with the excitement of the past ten days, I've already gotten out of the habit of exercising. Working out is not something I particularly like, but because I enjoy pizza and ice cream, going to the gym is something I force myself to do. Tomorrow, I promise. Tonight, I plan to have my own personal insanity evening.

Carefully, I select a red and open it so it has time to breathe. Meantime, I draw a nice hot bath. I enjoy a mindless debate between adding my lilac and chamomile petals or going with an orange-coconut–scented bubble bath before settling on the oil petals. Moments later, with my wine and magazine placed on the side of the tub and my big white terry bathrobe ready, I'm immersed in the hot water. It would be nice if my tub had pulsing jets, but I'm not complaining. It's long enough that I can stretch out with all of me underwater except my hands and head.

I subscribe to a lot of periodicals, but reserve two for reading during my nightly baths—a weekly one that offers snippets about TV stars and what will be on the tube that week and one that is purely a personality gossip magazine. As I settle down with the latter, it occurs to me that I exhibit another trait of my mother's. In my office, she told me she picked Reno because the movie magazines said it was *the* place for the stars to go for a quickie divorce. Those movie magazines were the precursor to

186

those I relish reading in the bathtub.

Turning to the short pieces at the front of the magazine, each featuring the photo of a beautiful person allegedly in love, pregnant, splitsville, or revealing a family secret, I try to read, but the warm water and luxurious oil quickly lull me into a half-sleep state. Luckily, I rescue the magazine before it gets soaked. Many times I fail to read an issue to the end because it becomes too wet and gross to dry out.

With my magazine saved, I give in to the urge for a catnap. My mind at first peacefully sorts craks, bams, and dots as I play Mah jongg with the Sunshine Village women in Heidi's apartment, but then my dream morphs and the other players become Vegas showgirls high kicking in beat to an insistent ringing. The dancers kick higher as the ring becomes more disturbing. It finally dawns on me that the sound is coming from my telephone.

I'm not even halfway out of the tub when it stops ringing. Because I don't recognize the caller ID, I take my time drying off, moisturizing, and putting on my robe. Only then do I listen to the message. Brian has something he wants to tell me. I immediately call him back, but I go straight to voicemail.

Retrieving my wine from the tub, I raise my glass as a toast. Tonight is mine.

CHAPTER FORTY-ONE

The office is abuzz when I arrive at work Wednesday morning. It takes me a few minutes to figure out what's happened. The something Brian may have wanted to tell me is that last night Chief Johnson personally arrested Lester Balfour. Rumors have the charges running from money laundering to fraud. Talk is split on whether his daughter, Barbara, also was arrested, or only detained for questioning.

Although I hang around the coffee machine to learn more, I quickly realize I have the gist of the story as my colleagues know it. To get the true scoop, I punch the return-call button, cross my fingers, and hope Brian answers. He does.

"If you're at the office," he says, "you probably heard we arrested Lester Balfour last night. We followed the money. He's allegedly been siphoning off some of the cash flow and double-dipping on drug and therapy billings."

"What about Barbara? Did you catch her hand in the till, too?"

"Not yet. It looks like larcenous Lester was two-timing his own daughter. We had her at the station last night, but that was to question her about Lindy Carleton's murder."

I'm sure Brian hears my intake of breath.

"We have a witness who puts her near the Riverwalk about the same time Lindy was taking her stroll. Of course, Barbara denies any wrongdoing."

"I have a hard time imagining Barbara on the Riverwalk, but

I guess if she was protecting her father or her job . . ."

"She claims she was looking for you."

"What?"

"She swears that when she realized the break-in was to your car and no one could find you in the building, she ran to check the garden and Riverwalk. She said she worried for your safety because the events of the past few weeks had her spooked."

"Hmmm. She may be telling the truth. She was so busy telling me how everyone was searching for me I had trouble making her understand Lindy needed help. Barbara couldn't seem to focus on what I was saying."

"We had her full attention at the station. She consistently repeated she went looking for you."

I remember the run in her hose and her soiled skirt. "Brian, I noticed that, for her, she was pretty disheveled."

"From her story, she has a logical explanation for that. She says she was in the parking lot with Officer Robinson until they got your car alarm turned off. When no one could find you, she claims she took the long way around the building to check the path to the Riverwalk by the stand of trees, but she slipped and fell on the unpaved part where it dips on the side of the building."

Even to suspicious me, what she says is believable. Unlike the other landscaped parts of the home, that side of the building, with a fenced-in place for the trash cans and a shed for the mower, is utilitarian. Beyond that, the part of the garden on the far side of the trees is undeveloped. Residents and guests rarely use the entrance through the trees. Instead, they tend to enjoy the Japanese garden or go through it to get to the Riverwalk.

"She could be telling the truth. It is pretty natural back there. That may explain how she got the run in her stocking, but what about knowing what her father was doing? Surely, she had to be in on that, too."

"Chief Johnson and I concluded we didn't have enough to hold her."

I hear noise in the background and Brian says he's got to run.

"One more thing, Brian. You've been giving a lot of time to Lindy's murder, so I was wondering if there's anything new on my mother's case?" He doesn't answer before the phone goes dead.

CHAPTER FORTY-TWO

Today is probably one of our last perfect Indian-summer days, and since I've heard as much of the gossip going around at work as I can stand, I decide to take Lester Balfour's advice and knock off early to spend some quality time with my father. I want to get a better handle on Lindy, my mother, the letter, and who else they might have known who might have hurt them or stolen the letter.

This time when my father isn't in his room, I don't panic. Instead, I look for him outside in the Japanese garden. It is easy to spot Carolyn and my father standing down by the thicket of trees that stand between the end of the garden and the almost-never-used second entrance to the Riverwalk. They wave at me to join them.

"What are you doing down in this area instead of over there in the Japanese garden?"

"We were checking the beehives," Carolyn says.

I frown, not understanding her. "Checking the beehives? What are you talking about?"

My father points through the stand of trees. "Our beekeeping group assured us that everything is back to normal now that the damaged racks have been repaired. We thought we'd take a look."

"Beekeeping group? Damaged racks? You mean the stinging bees weren't the ordinary ones flying around the garden?"

Carolyn laughs at my naiveté. "They were ordinary bees, that

191

our beekeeping group raises, but they don't usually sting. Do they Peter?" She holds his arm.

My father shakes his head.

"I'm completely confused."

"That's my role, honey." Carolyn and he laugh at his joke. "For the past couple of years," he says more seriously, "Sunshine Village has had a beekeeping group. We have hives, racks, and everything else we need to raise honey. We're careful and never had a problem with anyone getting stung until six months ago."

Seeing my surprise, my father tries to explain. "You know, like the Mah jongg group or the poker or bridge groups, we have a Sunshine Village beekeeping group. Carolyn used her research skills to help them get started."

"Consider it another one of my cheerleading things," Carolyn says.

I grin.

"Carrie, I know a lot of people dub my activities at Sunshine Village as falling under the cheerleading category, but just because we moved here doesn't mean we chose to stop living."

My father beams at her.

"I don't think you knew Charlie Roberts," Carolyn continues. "He died last year. When he moved into Sunshine Village, he was ready to die the next day. He never had kids and his wife had left him for another man so he was pretty lonely. A few of us worked to get him involved in anything. The old curmudgeon was having none of it until one of us found out about his interest in bees. Well, I checked out a bunch of books from the library, and with your father's help we found some folks to underwrite a few hives, bees, and beekeeping gear."

My father again points to the small stand of trees. This time I realize there is a well-trod path winding through them. "The Charlie Roberts Memorial hives are down the hill on the other side of those trees."

"I had no idea."

"Most people don't. Because almost everyone uses the first Riverwalk entrance from the Japanese garden or sits in the gazebo area in the main part of the garden, we put the beekeeping operation on this less-developed side beyond the trees to minimize people accidentally wandering by the hives."

"Bees are safe unless provoked," Carolyn adds. "We never had a problem with them until the day someone vandalized the honeycomb racks."

"Last week, when I had Shabbat dinner at Heidi's, Michael mentioned his wife was stung in the garden. Was she down by the hives?"

My father shakes his head. "No, she was actually working right near here when the hives were damaged." He points to a small flower bed planted on this side of the trees.

"Jess and the gardening club were doing some work in that bed. Someone threw a few of the racks into the stand of trees, smashing them. The provoked bees flew everywhere," Carolyn explains.

My father takes over telling the story again. "Jess was pushing some of the gardening-club members out of the way of the angry bees when she got stung a few times. Sadly, even though she had an epinephrine pen in a little knapsack nearby, in the confusion no one realized where the bag was. By the time Marta and Barbara got to her with another pen, it was too late."

"How horrible." I shudder as the three of us move away from the trees toward the middle of the Japanese garden.

"Bees don't like being messed with," Carolyn states in what I recall is her matter-of-fact library voice. She glances at me and then at her watch. "Why don't you two visit a bit? I need to do a few more things before dinner." I protest that she can stay, but, truthfully, as she leaves us, I'm glad for the time alone with my father.

I take his arm as we stroll through the garden entrance and along the Riverwalk. The temperature feels more like April than the beginning of November. "I swear the leaves have changed colors overnight. Aren't they gorgeous?"

"They are," he agrees, as he stops in front of a bench facing the water. "Too bad that when it rains tonight, so many of them will be washed to the ground." I'm surprised by my father's comment. A glass-half-full sentiment isn't his typical perspective.

He sits down on the bench and motions for me to do the same. I don't know what to say, especially when he continues, in the same vein. "I'm sure those leaves would like to stay there longer."

"I don't know what you're saying." Though I fear I have a glimmer.

He chuckles. "I'm rambling because I'm avoiding what I really want to talk to you about. It was so much easier for me to write it in a letter."

Now, I understand where this conversation is going. The letter. My father has finally decided to tell me what was in it. I've been mentally kicking myself all this time for not reading it when I had the chance. "You know, when I started to read the opening line, to 'My Dearest Daughter,' I thought Mother had written that. It's why I couldn't keep reading—not in the state I was in at the time."

"Carrie, I can't repeat it enough. Although I wrote the letter, either of us could have written 'My Dearest Daughter.' "

I nod, but don't answer him.

He looks away from me, out over the Wahoozee River. "I met your mother at a church social and we were married within six weeks."

Now, I am stunned. In all these years, my father has never spoken of their marriage.

"Six weeks?"

"Both of us immediately knew what we wanted." He smiles but quickly continues before I can interrupt him. "I had just come to Wahoo as a young, single minister. Everyone knew someone they wanted me to meet, but I was very prim and proper in those days. I explained I didn't want to date members of the congregation for fear of hurting someone's feelings if things didn't work out. The Women's Circle decided to get around that by holding a series of socials."

I imagine that our church matrons made sure every unmarried woman in town attended each social. "So, you met my mother at one of those?"

"Not until the third social. She walked in, very shyly—because other than the one friend who'd helped her get a job at the Wahoo library, Charlotte didn't know anyone. I saw her standing to the side of the doorway, with the sun playing in her red hair, and I went to welcome her. In some ways, you might say she was 'safe' because she wasn't a member of the congregation. Or, you could say I was so smitten that my resolve went out the window. Either way, we started dating. On our fourth date, I asked her to marry me."

"And she agreed that quickly?"

"No. She refused. Charlotte didn't think she was cut out to be a minister's wife because she hadn't been brought up in a religious household. Her father, who'd been married twice, didn't believe in organized religion and her mother, who died when Charlotte was ten, had acquiesced to having no religion in their home."

"That didn't mean my mother couldn't learn."

"My argument exactly. Your mother was smart, good with people, caring—all the traits for my congregation to love her. And after we were married, they did."

"But she didn't love them?"

"Carrie, easy. If you make assumptions too quickly, you often jump to a wrong conclusion. In fact, your mother loved the members of our congregation."

I don't want to disagree with my father, but a good minister's wife wouldn't walk away from the flock, the minister, or her own daughter.

"When she was pregnant with you, she participated in the knitting group, visited the sick, was active in the Women's Circle, and still worked part-time at the library. After you were born, I convinced her to stop working outside of her church activities. Maybe that was a mistake."

"It wasn't like she was doing all the church activities in your name. With everything she had going on, how could that be a mistake?"

"Because indirectly her identity still became an extension of me. Couple that with what I now think probably was a bit of postpartum blues, and she became very suggestible. Somehow, Charlotte got it in her head that she couldn't be a southern minister's wife because she discovered she was Jewish."

"Excuse me?" I wonder if my father is telling me a factual story or if this is some new kind of delusional rant related to his dementia.

"I know you think this sounds crazy, especially since your mother always knew your grandmother didn't practice any religion, but shortly before your mother left us she found out her mother had been born Jewish. I've never known how she found this out or why she became absolutely obsessed with the fear her background would hurt my career and indirectly harm you."

Now I understand. I've read enough about comparative religions to know when a mother is Jewish, her children are considered Jewish. If what my father is saying about my mother's obsession is true, she'd have feared that some people in our southern congregation might have shunned her and then tried to discredit my father's ministry. The reality is that there always is someone who doesn't like the clergy. "Couldn't we have moved from the south and avoided any problem affecting your work?"

"I suggested precisely that, but your mother felt it would follow us to any pulpit I assumed. She left so it wouldn't ever be an issue for you or for me."

For a moment, I wonder why she would have thought it would have been a problem for me—until I again recall that in Judaism, the child of a Jewish mother is a Jew. That means, if my grandmother was Jewish, my mother was Jewish and I technically am Jewish, too. I stare at my father as I try to grasp the overall meaning of this.

"So, what you're saying is that in one sense, my singing in the choir, attending Wednesday and Sunday services, and even participating in Consecration and Confirmation were . . . were shams?"

"Of course they weren't shams."

My father reaches for my hand, but I pull away. "All these years, why didn't you tell me the truth?"

"I always told you the truth. I taught you to pray, to have a faith, and to care for people. These values are a part of all religions. What I wanted you to know and wrote in that letter is that whatever religion you choose to follow isn't important. The importance is that you follow what you believe in."

I am so stunned I barely hear what my father says next. Perhaps there is a valid reason that I never felt totally comfortable in my religious skin but I ban those thoughts from my head as I try to focus on what my father is saying.

"A lot of things happened when your mother left and when she had her accident. Maybe the decisions each of us made weren't right . . ."

"Not by a longshot." My head is spinning. Normally I feel calm when I look out at the water, but today the flow of the river mimics my own inability to be still.

"Carrie, I know now it wasn't right for me to do nothing more than write a letter for her to give you when she was ready, but I felt honor bound to respect Charlotte's sacrifice, especially when she promised she would come back someday to tell you the truth."

"How long were you going to wait? Twenty-six years from the time you wrote that letter to now is a long time to have done nothing."

"Carrie, what I wrote in my letter after your mother's accident is exactly what I told you today, and what I've lived as an example for you all these years. The letter details that my faith and ministry work for me, and hopes that faith will bring you peace, but tells you it doesn't matter what religion you choose. The only thing that matters to me, and to you, is that you conduct your life with integrity. Whatever you do, you will always be 'my dearest daughter.' "

At these words, I put my head on my father's shoulder and cry. I cry because I love him, because I believe him, and because I don't understand why my mother couldn't have shown her love for us by staying. I also cry because I'm not sure I have the ability to understand and totally forgive my mother's actions.

CHAPTER FORTY-THREE

We sit on the bench for a long time. We sit until I run out of tears and we run out of words. My father has just changed my life, but as the sun sets and a chill sets in, I can see as I walk him back to the building that he seems more at peace than he has in a long time. Again, he asks me to stay for dinner, but I can't face the dining room tonight. Instead, I kiss him and tell him I need a little time to sort things out.

Once he has gone into the building, I don't feel like driving to an empty apartment or walking all the way back to the River-walk, so I opt for the peace and orderliness of the Japanese garden. I curl up on the wall in the garden near the graceful red bridge. The stones of the wall still hold the warmth of the day's sun.

I don't know how much time passes as my mind keeps turning over the ironies of my family's dynamics that I am too emotionally raw to really process. Intellectually, I know that what my father told me doesn't change who I am. Cognitively, I understand that I am now different in that I have historical and new facets to explore, adopt, or reject.

"A penny for your thoughts?" Michael's voice startles me. I lose my balance on the wall, but he catches me before I fall. "Hey, easy. We don't want a re-enactment of Humpty Dumpty here." As he pulls back from his rescuing embrace, I can't help but smile at being compared to Humpty Dumpty. I may not have all the king's men at my service, but I should be able to prevent breaking into pieces. "Are you okay? You look like you've been crying."

"Allergies, but thank you for asking."

Michael bends to retrieve the book he dropped when he reached out for me. Although the Riverwalk lights are on, the only light in the garden is from spotlights attached to the building. I am about to comment that there definitely is not enough light to read his book when I remember this is where he comes to sit when he's thinking about Jess.

As I stand and move aside so he can claim the wall, I point to the book. "Bad night?"

"A little," he admits.

"Want to talk about it?"

"Not really. I miss Jess tonight." He moves over so I can share the wall with him.

"Any special event today?"

"No, not a birthday, anniversary, or anything like that. I went to talk to my former law firm and Jaimie Carleton about the phosphate report you found." Seeing how startled I am by what he is saying, he quickly puts my selfish fears about him having loose lips to rest. "I didn't tell anyone where I got the report, only the circumstances under which the legal discovery process was tampered with. Having the report itself gave me credibility."

He acts more confident and lawyerlike tonight than he has at any time except when he represented Marta. "Did you get your job back?"

"No, and I doubt I will." He grins again. "Even if Goram & Davis were to offer it to me, I don't want to be their collections manager again."

"So, why did you go talk to them?"

"To convince them not to dismiss the lawsuit. The phosphate report proves that Lindy's supposition was correct."

"I would think Jaimie would be your best ally."

"She may be, but she wants time to think over how this should be handled." He shrugs. "Maybe I'm the bull in the china shop, but I think we should go for the jugular."

"And she doesn't?" I wonder if a settlement is being brokered. If so, who stands to win from it? I pose the question to Michael, but he is as clueless as I am. Maybe blood will be thicker than water or maybe honesty will win the day, but we do agree that family dynamics will definitely be a factor in what happens.

As we talk about family dynamics, it's my turn to have loose lips. Despite my resolve to keep the information my father shared with me secret, I can't. I tell Michael everything. Then I ask him, "How does it feel to be Jewish?"

"It is what it is. It's all I've ever known." He laughs before realizing how serious I am. "Over the years, I've encountered stereotypical jokes and remarks that weren't the kindest, but I'm comfortable in my skin. Jess and I . . . um, I want Molly to be committed to our faith, too." He looks down at his book. "I have to tell you, without Jess to help me, I worry about that."

I look at him with my eyebrows raised because I'm not sure what he worries about. Maybe he worries that she lacks the guidance of a mother. Instead of assuming, I ask. "I don't think I understand."

"Molly is getting to an age where she questions everything and where she suffers little hurts with righteous indignity. This is the year non-Jewish children her age start Bible studies. Their churches create environments in which it's fun to get together after school and do things like going to services, tithing, and being part of a church-based community. In our community, some of us attend services and honor our traditions, but the reality is that we get our biggest turnout for the high holy days. When Molly's Christian friends begin their Bible study groups, but she's not invited, she won't understand why. These are the same kids she's played with for years."

I shudder, but I'm not sure if it's because I'm getting cold or remembering how involved I became when I started Bible study. And he is right. I remember how we left out the children who didn't share our faith. We didn't invite them to our church-sponsored skating and movie activities or later to our retreats and Sunday school classes. We all became immersed in the youth activities of whatever church or synagogue we belonged to. I may have played poker in the choir loft, but I played it with kids who shared my upbringing and were rebelling just like me.

Without my asking, Michael takes off his jacket and puts it around my shoulders. "Carrie, does what your father told you make you feel any different or is it just a matter of how you are processing the information?"

I'm surprised at how easily Michael cuts through my confusion. For the first time, without the guilt of my role in the discovery being botched and him being fired, I realize that he is far more than a collections lawyer. He backed himself into a living style based upon a certain salary, but now he has a chance to start anew.

In a way, it is the same for me. My mother's return and my father's letter have cast doubt on everything I believed about my past and family, but they also are offering me the opportunity to take stock of where I am and, if I choose, make a fresh start. The problem for me is that I don't know what direction I want to go in.

My career can take me anywhere, but, truth be told, I love the charm of Wahoo. The Riverwalk, the theater in the old train depot, the library, the marble courthouse and city buildings, and the suspended bridge are more than sketches to me. I may say I stayed here because of my father, but I also haven't looked for other work because Wahoo is as much a part of me as I am of it.

I don't know if that will change if I embrace my Jewish heritage. For that matter, I'm not sure I want to accept or acknowledge being Jewish and, yet, I have never felt that I fully belonged in my father's church. Perhaps that is why at different times in my life I examined atheism, beliefs based upon nature, and other styles of living. Unlike my understanding of my feelings for Wahoo, my religious background and my identification with my parents' beliefs will take longer for me to process.

"Speaking of families," Michael says, interrupting my rambling thoughts, "the Mah jongg group is upstairs in Mom's apartment. Want to snitch a piece of cake?"

I am about to say no, but then I'd have to give Michael back his jacket. It's gotten too cool out here to do that. Besides, chances are the cake is Mrs. Berger's. My stomach overrules my brain and I say, "How can I refuse such an offer? It beats the dinners they serve here."

"My sentiments exactly."

CHAPTER FORTY-FOUR

When Michael and I arrive upstairs, the first thing I do is grab a piece of paper towel from the kitchen roll to blow my nose. I hadn't thought about it when I was outside in the dark, but from the way Heidi is examining me in the harsh light of the apartment, my eyes and nose must appear red and runny.

"Carrie, are you coming down with a cold?" Carolyn asks.

Heidi keeps her eyes trained on my face as Michael and I respond together: "allergies." When Heidi asks me what I am allergic to, I mutter something in response. Maybe she's afraid of germs, or my red nose has lost me points in the "fresh meat for Michael" department—not that I care. He's a nice guy, but especially now, neither of us is ready for a new relationship. Besides, he's still in love with Jess.

Until we arrived, Lester Balfour's dishonest doings apparently had been the hot topic at the Mah jongg table. Satisfied that I am not contagious, the women resume discussing the various Sunshine Village services that declined because of his double-dipping at their expense.

"I feel sorry for Barbara," Hannah says, discarding a 7 bam.

Karen isn't buying into that. She tosses a 4 dot while challenging Hannah. "How can you feel sorry for her? She's the one who's been cutting the quality of our food!"

Ella calls the 4 dot and as the players exchange tiles, Ella cackles, "Now we know why there have been fewer tomatoes in the salad I order for Friday nights. When I complained that it

204

seemed skimpy and the price had gone up, Barbara told me the lack of tomatoes was because they were out of season but now we know she really was too cheap to buy them!"

"But she was trying to make ends meet," Hannah responds. "She had no idea what her father was doing."

"I'm not so sure of that," Heidi says, declaring Mah jongg. Unlike the time I played, everyone pays up. Before they can start another hand, Heidi announces it's time for cake. "Who wants coffee? How many decaf?"

While Heidi pours, Karen again does the cake honors.

"Thank you," I say to Carolyn, who jumps to serve me a cup of coffee before I can get it myself.

As we savor our pound cake, Hannah explains that she feels sorry for Barbara because no matter how old one is, it hurts to have your father deceive you. I don't even have to look at Michael, next to me on the couch, to feel the sideways glance he gives me. Mentally, I agree with Hannah, but I don't say anything. That is another thing I will have to work out. I'm hurt, but my love for my father is not diminished, simply changed.

The conversation moves from Lester and Barbara to the relationship between Lindy and Carleton IV. "Family dynamics always provide good conflict," Carolyn points out. "Just think of all the television shows that week after week pit brothers against each other or parents against children. It is an age-old theme in literature."

"True," Hannah responds, "but you can avoid the pain of TV families by changing the channel. In real life, a bad decision or an unkind word can ruin a life."

"But," Carolyn says, "sometimes the conflict can't be avoided. Look at Lindy and her son. Their value systems were just too different for them to co-exist peacefully."

"Maybe," Michael observes. "But there were issues like not

polluting the environment that they should have been able to agree on instead of Fourth spreading false rumors about his mother."

Tonight, I don't think I will be able to listen to too much more of this. Still, as each woman adds a comment about families in general or her own in particular, I realize not only how common the topic is for each of them, but how their years of friendship have shaped their tolerance for each other's viewpoints.

"Maybe all of you really are related to George Washington," I suggest.

"What makes you say that?" asks Carolyn. Before I can answer, Michael tells her the story of how Jess inputted the Maj group's data into a sample genealogy program that erroneously related all of them to George, the sample ancestor. Probably because Michael is telling the anecdote, all of us find it easier this time to laugh at Jess's mistake.

The "George Washington" story brings our dessert break to a good stopping point. While the players resume the game, Michael clears and I rinse the dishes before putting them in the dishwasher. As I bend over the dishwasher, carefully positioning china cups that I bet Heidi bought before Michael was born, I can't help thinking about my own family's connections. "Michael," I ask while straightening up, "how many people at Sunshine Village did Jess do charts for?"

"Almost everyone," Ella's voice booms from across the open kitchen-living area, responding before Michael has time to answer. Her ability to keep up with the game as well as other conversations suggests that playing Mah jongg definitely helps her cognitive powers.

"I don't think she got as far as the third floor," Carolyn remarks. "She didn't do mine and I don't remember her doing your father's."

Karen adds, "She did all of ours twice and I know she did Marta's and Barbara's because—don't hold me to which one it was—one of them really did have a tie to George Washington."

"Really?" I'm a little skeptical.

Ella smiles at Karen. "Cross her heart and hope to die."

CHAPTER FORTY-FIVE

Michael and I leave his mother's place at the same time. We ride down to the lobby together and say good night, but I don't head to my car right away. As difficult as my father's revelation has been for me, I know he must be fretting over my reaction. I decide to take the elevator up again and pop my head in to say good night. He is leaning back against his pillows in his bed, eyes closed but clutching his Bible, so I'm not sure whether he is awake or asleep. I whisper, "Dad, are you awake? I came to say good night and to tell you I love you."

"Love you, too," he says, without opening his eyes. "I've been sitting here praying that I didn't hurt you too badly. I'm so sorry if I did."

I squeeze myself next to him on his bed so that I can cuddle close, like I used to as a child. He puts his arm around me and slips himself a little lower in the bed so I can rest my head on his chest. "I was afraid you'd be so angry with me . . ."

"Never. We're family." As I say these words, a thought crosses my mind. "Dad, did Jess Shapiro ever do your genealogy chart?"

"She started to, but she died before she finished it. A tragedy, so young."

"How do you know she started it?" I prop myself on my elbow so I can see his face better.

"Because she told me. We ran into each other in the lobby less than an hour before she went outside and got stung. She said she was putting the finishing touches on a few of the charts, but . . ."

"Thanks, Dad!" A quick kiss and I'm on my way, pulling my cell phone from my pocket even before I'm out of his door. The number isn't in my contact list, but if I'm lucky, I haven't deleted it from "recent calls."

My call is answered at the same moment the elevator arrives. Its door slides open and I nod to Carolyn and others getting off before I step into the elevator. My focus is on the voice in my receiver.

"This is Michael. I'm away from the phone, but if you'll leave your name and number after the beep, I'll call you back as soon as possible."

Frustrated, I barely give the beep time to finish. "Michael . . . Carrie. Call me back whatever time you get this message. I've got an idea, but I need your help."

CHAPTER FORTY-SIX

Michael doesn't call before I go to bed and while I want to dial his number again, I restrain myself, figuring he'll return my message in the morning. As the hours pass the next day at the office, I'm so anxious for my phone to ring that I can't concentrate. Although I am uncertain of what I'm looking for, last night's conversation on genealogy and my father's revelations have me thinking about family connections.

I know I'm related to my father, and Barbara is related to her father, and a lot of folks at one time appeared to be distant relatives of George Washington, but I wonder if Jess's research revealed any other Wahoo family ties. In a small community like this, surely there are some relationships that none of us are aware of.

If anyone comes into my office today, it will be obvious that I am shortchanging CI. Instead of working on my dry tax assignments, I am surfing the net trying to figure out how to pinpoint family connections I only have a gut feeling about. For years genealogy was painstaking work, but the explosion of search engines has shrunk the world. My problem is I don't exactly know what I'm looking for, but I now understand how Jess was able to do genealogical charts for so many of Sunshine Village's residents.

Because of my mother, I hope my father is correct that Jess did most of his chart before her death. Even if she didn't give it to him, the draft has to be somewhere. I'm betting it is in a folder on her computer. I need to get into her program files to see if I can find my father's family tree. Not only will it document his lineage, it should have some breakdown of my mother's family lines. I probably will have to do more research, but I desperately hope I can find out something about my mother that will give me a starting point to better understand why she was never a part of my life—and, perhaps, a better understanding of who I really am.

When my cell phone finally rings, I answer on the first ring. "Michael?"

"Um, no. Brian."

Brian may not be able to see me, but I bet he knows my face is turning red from the flustered way I start explaining that I am waiting for Michael's call.

"Well, I don't want to keep you."

"Brian, it isn't like that." I know I should be annoyed by his petulant tone. Instead, I feel compelled to explain my family ancestry idea to gauge his reaction. Other than my father, Brian is the only person in my life I've ever bounced ridiculous ideas off of and felt comfortable while doing it. He approaches thorny issues in such a logical way that he makes me examine things from every angle.

When we lived together, there were plenty of times he didn't agree with my ultimate conclusions, like when I decided law school rather than the police academy was the better choice for me. He was disappointed I had come so far and was going to drop out. Still, he never tried to sway my decision—only to make me focus on all sides of the issue.

Brian will tell me truthfully if he thinks my idea of checking the family trees Jess charted is a good idea to find some leads as to who murdered Lindy and my mother, or simply a way of disguising my selfish motivation to understand myself through the development of my family tree.

As Brian responds to my explanation, I realize how much I have missed our ying-yang debates. "If Michael has Jess's computer, would you like me to help you check out your family connections?" he offers.

"Yes."

I am amazed how thrilled I am that he validates my idea and is willing to help me learn about my roots.

"You know, Red," he says with a quickening of his speech, "the odds are Jess kept the charts she did all in one place— probably on her computer. If Michael will allow us to go through all of her genealogical folders, we might find some other unexpected connections."

"You mean, like when I found out Lester and Barbara were father and daughter?"

"Exactly. In a small town like Wahoo, there are bound to be family ties going way back that were destroyed by bad blood."

I laugh. Wahoo is such a peaceful town. It has an old time square, marble courthouse, Riverwalk, and so many other amenities. Folklore about the Indians who originally settled Wahoo is widespread, but I have never heard of any McCoy-Hatfield–type situations.

"Hold on, Brian," I say into the telephone. "Instead of calling me back, Michael is just now sticking his head in my office."

Covering the receiver with my hand, I ask Michael: "What are you doing here?"

"I've come to take you dancing to the stars with me. Or at least to the eighth floor." The eighth floor is where Fourth's office is. That's the last place I want to go.

As Michael does a little soft-shoe number that ends with his arms spread out, I wonder if I should call security. Instead, I tell Brian, "I think I'm going to need to call you back when I find out about Jess's files. It may take a few minutes because Michael is dancing." I hang up and ask, "Michael, what's going on?"

"Lindy won!"

"That's nice." Now, I'm sure I should call security. "Lindy is dead. She can't win at anything."

"You're not following me."

"You have *that* right."

He sits in the same guest chair last used by Lester Balfour and puts a copy of a document on my desk. My eyes scan it quickly and the pieces begin to fit together. "Fourth has resigned?"

"Yes!" Michael smiles like a Cheshire cat. "Jaimie used the phosphate test report you found to track down the other testing. That's what she's been doing the last few days. I've got to tell you, that woman is sharp."

I'm sure she is. I feel a momentary pang of jealousy over his admiration of her, but I quickly dismiss it.

"Once she gained enough ammunition," he continues, "she went to some friends on the executive board to plot how to use it. They fashioned a plan knowing that a Lester-driven Carleton IV would divide the board votes. She wanted to avoid a stalemate."

"Effectively meaning Fourth and Lester would win."

"Right. Chief Johnson's arrest of Lester changed the entire playing field. Think of Carleton as a running back who makes some great plays, but take away the quarterback and he can't move the ball. Jaimie and her friends simply went in for the kill and Carleton backed down."

"I wouldn't think he'd simply give up. That's too easy a resolution."

"I would have thought so, too, but Jaimie convinced him by explaining the legal ramifications in terms of possible prison time for the pollution violations and the shady 'discovery' practices. Carleton decided that being Lester's roommate wasn't very appealing. He is, as we speak, giving a press conference declaring his health dictates the need for an immediate and permanent retirement and that he is turning over the reins of Carleton Industries to his daughter, Jaimie."

"That still doesn't make the pollution go away."

"No, that will take time, but Jaimie is willing to put CI's money and power behind doing the right thing for the river. She really does believe Carleton Industries has an obligation to be a good corporate citizen."

Suddenly, I have a sinking feeling. "Did she offer you a job in this new regime? A chance to be in charge of cleaning this mess up for Carleton Industries?"

"Yes, she did make me an offer."

I know I am frowning, but I can't bring myself to smile at this turn of events. I don't know Jaimie, but I am afraid she will bring him on board to effectively silence him.

"Jaimie wants things done the way Lindy had in mind," Michael explains.

I focus my eyes on the framed pictures on my wall. This is a time I should be gracious in my comments, but my brain can't control my tongue. "Let me see . . . um, she told you that because you had worked so closely with Lindy and had an honest vision, you were the best person to see Carleton Industries' environmental changes through."

"Pretty much something like that, but I didn't take the job."

I am surprised.

"I suggested she already had someone with proven integrity on her staff who'd be far better than I would at supporting her vision to make CI a good corporate citizen. I'd rather be the neutral fly on the wall making sure CI and others do what's right." He waits for me to eventually understand what he's saying. "She wants to see you at three." While he continues talking,

I glance from him to my computer screen to see if a meeting has been added to my calendar. It has.

"When we were at the Fattburger, do you remember asking me what I liked and might want to do?" He doesn't wait for me to acknowledge remembering our conversation. "I'm a sucker. The paycheck from the firm was nice, but I think Molly and I can get by on a nonprofit salary. I may join the environmental group I was helping pro bono or I may put out my own shingle; but I promise you, I'll be a watchdog on Jaimie's tail." He does another little dance step.

I hate to dampen his excitement. "Michael, I need to ask you a totally unrelated question." He stops dancing. "Did Jess use a computer for doing her genealogical research and charts?"

"Her laptop."

"Do you still have it?"

"At home. Why?"

"I've a hunch that family connections may be what we're overlooking. Going through her charts might help me learn more about my family and might even help Brian, you, and me figure out who killed Lindy and my mother."

CHAPTER FORTY-SEVEN

"Do you see what you're looking for?" Brian stands over my shoulder. Michael, who sits across his dining room table from me, also waits expectantly. I called Brian to join us. If we find a connection between any of the residents that makes sense to him, this could become a police matter.

"No, I don't. Jess finished only the paternal side of my father's chart." I point to the generations leading to my father's birth and the horizontal line showing his marriage to my mother, Charlotte Harper. A vertical line from their union traces my be-gat lineage, but none of the details of my mother's family. "This doesn't help me know anything more about my mother. We're back to where we started with the same suspects: Marta, Barbara, and all the residents of Sunshine Village." I push the laptop away from me, disappointed and discouraged.

Michael pulls the computer toward him. "It's only eleven o'clock. Let's see who else Jess charted. We've got time. Jaimie can't see you before three and I don't have to get Molly from school until then."

Brian moves to stand behind Michael's shoulder as Michael exits from my father's chart and goes back to the program files. "Is there an index or some kind of spreadsheet?" Brian asks.

"I don't think so. Looks like Jess only used initials to name each file."

I have come around the table and now peer over Michael's other shoulder as he opens one marked *BB*. Michael clicks on it and Barbara Balfour's chart opens. We each lean in to see who Jess connected her to, but it isn't a particularly exciting lineage as none of us recognize any names except for her father, Lester.

Michael closes the *BB* file and moves to one whose initial is an *M*. The file belongs to one of the men who lives on the fifth floor of the building. He next opens an *H* file. It is Carolyn Holt's, but except for her name and where Jess notated Deborah Holt tied to a line with an *H*, it is blank. Carolyn apparently was right; Jess didn't finish the third-floor charts.

Exiting, Michael opens another folder. I let out a low whistle as I read the connecting lines. "According to Jess, Marta can trace her family tree back to the Randolphs." Brian and Michael both give me a "so what" look as they wait for me to explain my excitement. I point so they can follow my finger to a line that shows Martha Randolph's name above that of twelve children, eleven of whom survived into adulthood and had children. "Do you see who *Martha's* father was?"

"Really?" Brian asks.

"The Mah jongg group had it wrong."

"So, what's new about that?" Michael mutters.

I ignore him. "Marta isn't related to George Washington. Instead, she is a direct descendant of Thomas Jefferson through his daughter Martha Jefferson Randolph. How about that?"

"*That's* the kind of thing Jess really enjoyed finding when she did someone's chart—unexpected relationships. But, I don't think a connection to Thomas Jefferson has too much bearing on our Wahoo murders."

"I can see why Jess got a kick out of this, though," Brian says. "This genealogy stuff can be pretty high-powered stuff."

Leaving Marta's chart, Michael randomly opens and closes other files. Although some of the people and a few of the staff members at the nursing home are relatives, close and distant, nothing Michael finds gives us a motive for murder.

No longer reading over Michael's shoulder, Brian says, "It doesn't look like anything supports your theory, Red."

Dejected, I have to agree. "Well, thinking that Jess stumbled onto an unexpected family connection was a good hypothesis. Too bad it didn't work out. Do you two want to get a late lunch?"

CHAPTER FORTY-EIGHT

Even though I've been killing time since Michael and I had lunch—Brian having begged off—three o'clock comes too soon. Michael may be dancing about Jaimie's brilliance and how she used the paper I found, but I think he's naïve. She hasn't been in her new position long enough to be promoting people. As smart as she is, it probably hasn't taken much for her to jump from his suggesting that I might be a good person for the clean-up job to figuring out I stole the testing report from CI. My retrieving the report from the floor isn't protected by any kind of privilege, so I'm pretty sure, once she calls me into her office, she'll fire me on the spot for stealing company property.

As I sit in what was Fourth's outer office, I look around. The room has a different feel than the last time I entered it. The same leather couches and wood-paneled walls still evoke a boardroom mentality, but flowers in a vase on the receptionist's desk and sitting on the coffee table make the waiting area more inviting. A different receptionist from the one who was here last Monday apologizes that my appointment will be delayed for about ten minutes because Ms. Carleton's London conference call started late. She offers to get me a cup of coffee and when she brings it to me, she assures me that it should only be a few more minutes.

I barely finish half of my coffee when Jaimie bounds out of her office, her black hair pulled back into a simple, bouncing ponytail. "So sorry to keep you waiting," she says, inviting me into her inner sanctum. "I've been spending most of today touching base with all of our management teams. It's great to be able to hold virtual meetings, but catching everyone in their different time zones is a real bear."

I have no fear that Jaimie will quickly get the hang of it. She hit the ground running, and obviously is making her presence known. In the hour I was waiting to come upstairs, there was a buzz of palpable excitement on my floor about the leadership change. Me, I refrain from judgment. For my father's sake, I only pray I still have a job when this meeting is over.

She still has Fourth's furniture in her private office, but the atmosphere in there has changed, too. Unlike her father, who put his massive desk between us during our meeting, Jaimie takes the guest chair next to me.

"Ms. Martin," she begins.

"Carrie," I interrupt.

"Carrie, it is. First, I want to thank you for helping to clear the stigma that my father tried to associate with my grand-mother. As you know, she left a legacy to the public that it was never aware of." Jaimie glances at a picture of her grandmother sitting on the corner of her desk. "As much as I want to correct people's perception of my grandmother, I know that isn't where she would want me to focus my attention. Not at this time, for sure."

Jaimie's words evidence how deeply she cared for Lindy. I am lucky that when my mother left, my father had the desire and willingness to parent me. He may not have gotten everything right all the time, but I never had grounds to question his love for me. Maybe if Jaimie had been a basset hound, her father would have appreciated her more, but there's no question her grandmother stepped up to the plate.

Watching Jaimie in action, I think I am seeing what Lindy Carleton must have been like as a young woman. As much of a dynamo as Jaimie is, the loss of her grandmother has to have taken its toll on her.

"Carrie, are you happy at Carleton Industries?"

"Happy? I've never really thought about it, Ms. Carleton."

"Sure you have. You think of it every day you pull into the parking lot. Do you want to be here or does your whole mood change as you're parking? Are the weekends better than the weekdays?"

I squirm inside, trying to think of the best way to answer her questions. Who knows if it is Sunday or Wednesday? I've been putting in the same amount of hours 24/7. "My mood is stable whether I'm in the building or the parking lot, and it really doesn't matter which day of the week it is because I often work all of them."

"That's not right. Our people deserve downtime to spend with their families or do whatever they want."

"But what about the work?"

"If we're a family-oriented company treating our employees right, the work will get done. For the past few years, while abroad, I've studied numerous productivity models. The best ones seem to be interpretations of the Golden Rule."

I don't know if it is good or bad that she thinks best business practices should be based upon a biblical passage. People have said Jaimie is levelheaded, and Michael and the Mah jongg ladies think highly of her, but I am a little leery of how Carleton Industries will fare under her leadership. Rather than trying to directly see if she is a zealot, I make a more innocuous comment. "I think you'd get along well with my father."

"That's what I've heard. I also understand you and I should be able to hit it off."

"Sounds like you've been talking to my press agent."

She smiles at that. "I wish I could hire that agent."

It's my turn to politely laugh. I sense we are reaching the

crux of this meeting. "Carrie, I've been looking over your record," she says, randomly waving her hand toward her desk. There are a few thin files lying there so I presume one is my personnel file. She probably had it pulled so she can document this meeting and the reasons she plans to fire me. "Your talents are being wasted at Carleton Industries." Great. Michael intimated she was going to promote me and here I am getting axed.

"For that matter," she says, pointing specifically at the folders on her desk, "a lot of our young employees are not being allowed to reach their potential. They are either becoming mediocre employees or leaving for other opportunities." She lets that sink in for a moment. Although I could agree with her because I have seen the revolving door with my friends, I hold my tongue.

"I don't want that to continue. I'd like you to help me do something about this problem."

Good. If I'm helping, I can't be being fired. I stop sweating. "What do you have in mind?"

"I know you have other responsibilities, but I'd also like you to work with me on a Strategic Planning and Human Resources project. Before we restructure anything, we've got to figure out what we've got and where we need to go. I want you to chair the project."

I'm taken aback. Not a promotion or the job I expected to be offered, but she's definitely not firing me. "Ms. Carleton . . ."

"Jaimie."

". . . you're going to have enough to contend with. Don't you think someone with more seniority and expertise would be able to help you better than I could?"

"Perhaps, but you can put that kind of person on your project team. Right now, if Carleton Industries is to successfully change with the times, we need to take it in a new direction. You've done that before, so I know you understand what I'm talking about."

Not sure what she is referring to, I wait for her to explain further.

"When you dropped out of the police academy and then opted for law school, you made an educated lifestyle decision."

"Not everyone would agree with you."

Jaimie laughs. "I got some of the same reaction when I announced that instead of working on Wall Street, I was coming back to Wahoo, Alabama. For you to have put in the training it took to make the police academy and then to decide on your own terms it wasn't right for you demonstrates self-knowledge and personal courage. I respect that and truly believe that together we can come up with a team that can create a workable strategic plan."

"I'm willing to give it a shot."

"Good," Jaimie says. She leans back, never taking her piercing, chocolate eyes off mine. "Teamwork is going to help me keep a part of my grandmother alive. Any other questions?"

"By any chance, can we hold the team meetings in an office as nice as this one?"

Chapter Forty-Nine

Walking out of Jaimie's office, I am thrilled to not only still be employed, but to have an opportunity to help CI build for the future. Maybe I also can strategically help plan a more interesting role for me in Carleton Industries, but, for today, I am simply grateful to have a job. My conversation with Jaimie about employees having to make time to be engaged in family and personal activities really hit home.

Criminal or not, Lester Balfour was right about one thing. I need to spend as much quality time with my father as I can, but Jaimie's correct, too—I have to develop a life that isn't consumed by CI or by my father's illness. It's easy to talk about striking a balance between work and my personal life, but it is going to require me to make some real changes in the way I do things.

I don't think I'm ready to be a regular Mah jongg player, but I envy the friendship and loyalty the Sunshine Village players have for each other. Even though Jess's genealogy charts don't show it, they are as much a family as my father and me or Heidi, Michael, and Molly. I feel sorry for people who don't reach out to others to create family units.

Sitting down in my office chair, with a cup of coffee, I think about how I shared coffee over this very desk with my mother. What kind of relationship might we have had if someone hadn't cut her life short?

My mother was murdered almost two weeks ago, but Brian

doesn't seem any closer to finding her killer or to figuring out why anyone would break into my car to steal a letter.

Blood relations or not, connections are key. Take Carolyn: she could have been alone, but she's happy with the family she has created. I know I love her and she loves me, but from my end, it isn't quite the same.

Carolyn feels all of us are her adopted family and she certainly tried to fill in in so many ways for my mother, but we never developed the bond I have with my father. It has to be the same with all the children she helped at the library or the activities she runs at Sunshine Village: everyone at some point prioritizes their own families and she pretty much is left alone. I don't want that kind of life for myself. I don't want an empty family tree. Nor do I want a family like Jaimie's that can be carefully traced on paper but is empty of real connections.

That's it! Empty tracings—that's what I missed when Michael, Brian, and I were reviewing the charts Jess did. Instead of direct connections, we need to go back and look for empty or broken connections. Maybe there *is* a subtle Hatfield vs. McCoy rivalry in Wahoo.

CHAPTER FIFTY

It isn't quite six when I arrive at Sunshine Village. I shared my relationship hunch with Brian and he thought it had merit so we hatched a plan. Brian called Michael to ask him to bring Jess's computer to Heidi's and to have her arrange for everyone—Marta, Barbara, the other Mah jongg players, and me—to meet at her apartment at six. We doubt we will get a Perry Mason style confession but hope that if Michael pulls family charts up on Jess's computer and Brian and I play a modified game of twenty questions—colored by a little bad cop/good cop behavior—the three of us can figure things out without anyone else getting hurt.

Because I'm early, I decide I have time to poke my head into my father's room. He sits in his chair, patient as always, listening to Molly read *Goodnight Moon*. I blow him a kiss that he acknowledges by touching his cheek, but neither of us interrupts Molly's reading. I duck back into the hall, thinking it best to leave the two of them occupied by one of my all-time favorite books while I go upstairs to Heidi's apartment.

For once, Karen didn't have time to whip up something lovin' from the oven. She is unwrapping a store-bought cake. I take mental attendance of who is in the room. Carolyn and Hannah are missing.

Everyone, even Ella, who floats back and forth between Brian and Barbara, is antsy. "Can we start yet?" she demands.

Michael looks up from the table where the Mah jongg set

usually is. Today, he is using the table for his computer station. The Maj tiles and racks must be in the battered case under the card table.

"It's just past six," Brian says, glancing at his watch. "Let's give Carolyn and Hannah a few more minutes to get back before we start."

I realize from his comment that they must already have been here. "Where are they?" I ask.

"They were here, but you weren't," Ella proclaims. Her tone lets everyone know that the show could have gotten on the road earlier if I'd come upstairs when Michael and Brian did. "Marta was telling all of us how the laundry returned *Goodnight Moon* after it got mixed in with your father's sheets, and that reminded both of them that this evening is dirty-laundry collection time. They went back downstairs to put their laundry bags out for pickup."

"I was telling them," Marta explains, standing to the side, probably unaccustomed to being included in a meeting like this, "how I noticed the book still on the shelf at the third floor nurse's station when I went by a little while ago, so I dropped it off at your father's room before coming upstairs. Molly was with your father and she immediately decided to read it to him."

"Thanks. She was reading it to him when I stopped by his room."

Ella snorts, but I don't apologize for keeping everyone waiting for me. Considering what the next few minutes will bring, it was nice to see Molly reading *Goodnight Moon* to my father.

Speaking of *Goodnight Moon*, I notice a framed photo of Molly on the end table next to the couch. I pick it up and turn it over in my hands. "My father adores the time she spends with him." I remember something else as I look at the picture. "Oh, my, Hannah and Carolyn? No!"

Karen holds a piece of cake out to me, but instead of taking it from her, I thrust the picture into her free hand. "Brian, Michael," I shout across the room, already moving toward the door. "We need to get down to my father's room. Now!"

"What is it, Red?"

"Hannah lives on the fourth floor, but Carolyn has a room on the assisted-living floor. Residents on assisted-living floors don't put their own laundry bags out. That's one of the 'assisted' services."

"So?" Karen demands, planting herself in front of me.

"The day my mother was killed, Molly was reading *Goodnight Moon* to my father. She said she found him holding the book repeating 'Carrie, read.' " I push myself around Karen to head for the door.

"She told me he only calmed down after she took *Goodnight Moon* from him and began reading it aloud. He didn't know me that day because of his urinary infection. He must have thought Molly was me and that when I began reading the book, I would see whatever he wanted me to know. That's why he calmed down and went to sleep while Molly was reading."

I don't feel there is time to wait for the elevator so I take the stairs. Michael and Brian follow me. We burst into my father's room. He is alone. "Where's Molly?" Michael shouts.

"Carolyn took her for a reading session. I was getting tired and she said you still were busy upstairs." I take in the entire room with one glance. There is no sign of the book that Molly was reading, but her little pocketbook sits on the window ledge.

Michael's eyes follow mine to the ledge.

In that instant, we both can guess, from Carolyn's family tree on Jess's computer, where she may have taken Molly. "The garden!" I yell at Brian.

Before following them, I grab Molly's purse and shout at my father, "Did my mother know Carolyn before you got married?"

"Of course. Carolyn was the friend who helped Charlotte get her job at the library."

CHAPTER FIFTY-ONE

Michael and Brian reach the Japanese garden ahead of me, but I have the advantage of knowing exactly where we need to go. "Down there!" I run toward the stand of trees with the beehives behind them, praying we reach Carolyn before she has time to provoke the bees.

I slow down as I approach the flat area at the edge of the Japanese garden. Through an opening in the center of the trees, I can see Molly perched about three feet off the ground in the crook of a small tree. She holds the *Goodnight Moon* book. Although I can't see Carolyn, I'm guessing from Molly's whimpering and the direction she is looking that Carolyn stands directly across from her, to my left, near the beehives.

Behind me, Brian motions Michael to circle around behind the stand of trees while he goes back through the main Japanese garden entrance to the Riverwalk and then re-enters the Sunshine Village property through the lesser-used entrance. That should bring him out above where Molly and Carolyn are.

As Michael picks his way gingerly through the uneven, muddy area on the far side of the trees, I realize Barbara definitely told the truth about having fallen while looking for me the other night. Even though she had no reason to suspect Carolyn, Barbara must have feared, as I do tonight, a repeat of the circumstances of Jess's death. Quietly, I make my way down the makeshift path the beekeeping club members have worn between the trees.

As I get closer, I see Carolyn wearing gloves and a beekeeper's veil. She stands in front of the hives talking calmly to Molly as if she is giving a learning lecture at the library. "Bees are nothing to be afraid of. They are our friends." Carolyn reaches into a hive with her left hand and pulls out a rack covered with honeycomb and moving, but peaceful, bees. "See, so long as we don't disturb them, they won't harm us."

Carolyn holds the rack out toward where Molly is perched, but Molly looks away. "I don't like bees. I want to go to Nana's." Carolyn makes a noise from her throat, but doesn't say anything as she takes a step closer to Molly.

Molly squirms, trying to wiggle out of the tree, but stops when she drops the book. She stiffens and leans back against the far side of the Y in the tree as she watches to see how the bees react to the sound of the book falling.

"Bees don't like whiners."

I move forward, trying to be silent, but my foot snaps a twig. Carolyn reacts to the sound by looking in my direction. No longer attempting to be quiet, I quickly step out from the stand of trees into the clearing. I put myself between Molly and Carolyn.

"Hello!" I say with mock joy. "What are you two up to?" My attempt to sound casual comes across as a little too cheerful, but there's nothing I can do about it except keep up the charade.

"You didn't need to come down here, Carrie," Carolyn says. "Your father looked so tired, I thought Molly and I could have another reading session while you had your meeting at Heidi's."

"Oh, that's okay. I came out here to find you. Nobody wanted to start without you." I bend down and pick up the fallen copy of *Goodnight Moon*.

"This was always my favorite book when my mother read to me," I say, dusting it off. I flip through the pages, looking for what, I don't know. Nothing jumps out and catches my eye.

"I'm sure you recommended it to a lot of young mothers who came to the library looking for books to read to their children."

"Of course. It's a classic."

"And I bet you gave it as a gift, too."

"Only in special circumstances. After all," she laughs, "a good librarian always recommends checking out books from the library's collection. It makes little readers want to come in again and again—even if they keep checking out the same book."

"You really understood being a children's librarian. You certainly taught me to love books." I open the cover and glance at the title page for a moment, before closing the book again, leaving my thumb in it as a placeholder. Ignoring Molly's sobbing, I look beyond the menacing rack of bees in Carolyn's hand to the other peaceful hives. I take a few steps closer to Carolyn, effectively using my body as a barrier between Molly and her.

"When my father and you told me the other day how you helped start the Charlie Roberts beekeeping project, I didn't realize you were so into it."

"Not so much since Charlie passed away."

"Coming up with the idea for this beekeeping area was really thoughtful of you. If I remember what you said, he was in a horrible state of mind after his wife left him, but from what I can see, you definitely gave him a reason to live again. I bet he considered each of these bees as a friend."

Carolyn doesn't say anything but she does look a little less agitated so I continue. "You really made a difference in his life, as you have for so many of the residents here. I'd hate to live here without children or family who care enough to visit." Realizing what I have just said, I hasten to add, "Or good friends who care enough to watch out for me."

"That's right. Without friends or family, it can be horrible to live here or anywhere." She tightens her grip on the rack, raising it a few inches. Even though it is only three feet from me, I consider the rack to be a giant barrier.

"Mr. Roberts wasn't as lucky as your mother, was he?" I say softly. "After your father left, your mother always had you, didn't she?"

"We had each other," Carolyn declares. "We didn't need him."

"Is that why you changed your last name to hers?" I wait to see how she will react, but her expression doesn't change.

"My mother, Deborah Holt, was a very special woman. After their divorce, she took her maiden name back. Because she made me who I am, I'm proud to carry on her name rather than the Harper name." She spits on the ground. "My father was trash and he left us to have a daughter with another piece of trash."

"Jess realized you changed your name, didn't she?"

Carolyn nods. "Jess started doing your father's chart. When she was researching your mother's lineage, Jess saw your mother had a half-sister. It didn't mean anything to her at first. If she had simply stopped at that point, she'd still be alive today." I block out Molly's sobs and keep my attention focused on Carolyn as she takes another step forward.

"Jess came to see me because she was confused as to why it appeared I went by Carolyn Holt when my mother's name was Holt, but my father's name was Harper. I tried to tell her she was mistaken, but she laughingly assured me that this wasn't a George Washington mistake. Jess had double-checked her research and knew she was correct, but she wanted my confirmation and an explanation so she could annotate the chart."

Carolyn glares at me. "You shouldn't have come down here, Carrie."

"I had to. The secret doesn't matter anymore."

"That's what your mother said." She shifts the rack to hold it with both hands. It doesn't look heavy, but the bees appear to be more awake.

"When did she say that?" My voice shakes as I force myself to tune out Molly's ragged crying.

Carolyn looks at me as if I am a fool. "When Charlotte came back to Sunshine Village after seeing you."

I say nothing. As with my mother, I realize Carolyn will tell me more if I wait patiently.

"Charlotte came by early in the day to ask your father how to find you. After they visited for a while, Charlotte told him good-bye and gave him the copy of *Goodnight Moon* you have in your hand. She kept the book and your father's letter all these years to give to you."

Now I know Charlotte must have dropped the piece of pipe cleaner when she opened her bag to leave the book with my father. "But if she said a final good-bye, why did she come back?"

"Charlotte came back the second time to tell your father she had given you the letter and now agreed with him that nothing stood in the way of her staying in Wahoo."

I am confused. My mother wanted to stay in Wahoo? "What are you saying?"

"After meeting you, Charlotte felt you would understand why she left. She wanted to try to build as much of a relationship with you as you would allow. I couldn't let her do that."

"Why?" I can't help but repeat myself. I keep my tone sounding curious rather than accusatory. "Why couldn't you let her stay in Wahoo?"

"Because Peter and you are *my* family, now."

I'm shocked to see this delusional side of someone I've considered a dear friend, almost a second mother. Her words may lack logic, but her demeanor is as if she is teaching a lesson at a lesson at the library. Did I miss seeing behaviors that might have warned me? I try to think when she stepped over the line of sanity, but, until this moment, other than her allegiance to family, I had no idea.

"But if you felt this way, why did you help her get a job at the library?"

"Back then, Charlotte reached out to meet me as my sister. I felt sorry for her when she told me her mother died when she was little and that she grew up with him. So, I took her under my wing. She needed a job and the library had an opening."

"That was just like you, kind and generous," I say soothingly.

Looking beyond her, I see Brian coming closer. I angle my body to keep her attention away from him. I'm uncertain where Michael is.

Carolyn laughs. "But she turned out to be a wicked thief just like her father. I took her to the social to meet Peter and she stole him away from me." I don't respond. If what my father told me is true, he never led Carolyn to believe he had any feelings for her. "Without Charlotte, Peter eventually would have been my husband and you might have been my real daughter."

The pieces begin to click. Except for my father, Carolyn is the only other person whom my mother really knew in Wahoo. "Did you convince her to leave us?"

"Yes."

"Why?"

"So Peter would be able to stay in Wahoo. Once I realized her mother was Jewish, it was easy to make her believe that if people found out you and she technically were Jewish, it would hurt Peter's career in a small town like this. That she could kill all of Peter's dreams."

"But they could have gone to a different city."

"I couldn't let that happen. I couldn't let my family go." She stops, listening, perhaps having heard Brian or Michael moving, but when all is silent, she continues. "I made her believe that it would be the same anywhere they moved. There would always be snickering whisperers who could hurt his opportunity to be the type of minister he envisioned."

I'm so shocked, I don't know what to say, but Carolyn no longer needs me to prompt her. "Everything would have been fine if Charlotte stayed away from Wahoo. Even if she had just seen your father and left, it would have been okay, but she came back from seeing you bubbling with excitement that there could be a place for her in Wahoo."

"So, you stabbed her?"

"Not then. I convinced Charlotte that, instead of going straight to Peter, she should surprise both of you by pretending to be me at the story hour. She loved the idea. We often took turns dressing up as characters for the children's reading hour at the library. It was easy to fool everyone by dressing up as each other because the two of us were built so similarly." She moves the rack back to her left hand. With her free right hand, she adjusts her beekeeping veil. "Your mother thought it would be like old times."

I now can clearly see the resemblance between my mother and Carolyn. "You talked her into putting on your coat and hat?"

"It didn't take any convincing. She loved the idea of surprising you." Carolyn shakes her head and slips into the library voice that makes me feel six years old. "She waited in my room while I went down to help Hannah. I wanted to make sure people saw me dressed in my Burberry outfit. Between the boots and buttoned coat, no one knew I didn't have anything under my coat except underwear." She pauses and smiles. "Charlotte and I had a good laugh about my needing to be careful so I didn't flash anyone."

I slip my thumb out from between the cover and front page of *Goodnight Moon.*

"When I got back to my room, your mother was waiting for me. She was so excited about surprising Peter and you that she barely let me get out of my coat and hat before she put them on and picked up my bag of treats."

"And that's when you stabbed her?"

Carolyn nods affirmatively. I look at the rack in her hand, swarming with bees. "You hit yourself?"

"With the Halloween festivities and all the visitors occupied downstairs, it was easy to wrap myself in a few towels and get to the linen closet. From years of helping children research all kinds of facts, I knew that if I hit myself hard enough near the temple, my bruise would really appear serious." She looks down at her left hand, which still grasps the rack. "I guess I hit myself a little harder than I needed."

"Yes, you did. Thank goodness you didn't hurt yourself worse."

Carolyn ignores my attempt to be kind to her. She holds her right hand out to me. "I think you best give me the book now."

At that moment, Brian comes through the entrance beyond the beehives while Michael crashes through from the tree-lined side of the clearing. Seeing them, Carolyn slams the rack against the ground.

"Get Molly!" I shout. Brian grabs Molly from her tree perch. She cowers in his arms as he retraces his steps away from the hives toward the Riverwalk.

Michael rushes toward Carolyn and shoves her away from the hives before she can pull another rack out. He yelps as bees sting him, but reaches out and yanks at her veil. The netting comes off in his hand. Free, she runs from him, throwing the part of the rack she still holds behind her. I stumble over it.

Bees sting my face and neck, but I follow her. My legs get heavy and I begin to sway. As my breathing becomes more labored, I fall to the ground gasping, "Michael!"

I see Michael look toward where Molly and Brian must be even as he turns back to me. He bends over me repeating my name while tugging at Molly's little purse still slung over my arm. I try to answer him, but can't through my closing throat. Bees continue to sting me. I barely force my eyes open to see the pink- and white-haired ladies causing a commotion behind him when I feel a sting in my thigh greater than any of the other bee stings. As everything around me goes black, it registers with me that the Mah Jongg players have perfectly played their hand against their fifth, my Aunt Carolyn.

CHAPTER FIFTY-TWO

When I wake up in my hospital room, my father is sitting, exactly like he must have sat next to my mother's hospital bed, holding my hand. He leans over to kiss me without letting go of the hand that doesn't have IV fluids running into it. "I'm sorry. I never realized Charlotte and Carolyn were half-sisters. I thought they were close friends."

I murmur something and look around the room. A bouquet of flowers and a balloon arrangement are on the windowsill. My father identifies the flowers as being from Brian and the balloons from Michael, Heidi, and Molly. I start to ask about everyone, but he hastens to assure me I don't have to worry about anyone or anything except getting well. He also tells me Carolyn has been committed to another type of hospital.

"Michael saved your life by using Molly's pen when you had the anaphylactic reaction to the bee stings." That explains why my thigh feels sore, but it doesn't explain why my father flits from subject to subject.

"It was Carolyn who got your mother a job at the library," he says. "I guess back then, most places didn't hire relatives. Even though they favored each other, because they didn't have the same last name, nobody realized they were related." He lets go of my hand. "I never did."

He pauses for breath or to remember the past. "Carolyn brought your mother to the church social and introduced us."

"It must have destroyed her when you fell for Charlotte."

"Carrie, I never thought of Carolyn in that way." I know my father is telling the truth. He probably was as kind to her as he was to everyone. Apparently, for all these years, he was as oblivious to her obsession with him as I was until Marta pointed it out to me the night everyone else was at Carolyn's impromptu welcome-home party. "How did you figure out they were related?" he asks.

"Two things. The similar vibes they gave off to me."

"Huh?"

"Molly told me she couldn't understand how I didn't recognize my mother. She insisted she would always have known her own mother. I thought about how many times I've seen Carolyn in her storytelling costume; yet, the sneakers instead of Burberry boots didn't jump out at me even the first few times I looked at the pictures I snapped. When it came to me that there had to be a reason I didn't find anything amiss, I realized my emotional reaction to my mother and Carolyn was the same."

"Women's intuition?"

"No, daughter's love. Carolyn served as a surrogate mother to me in so many ways. That's why I couldn't leave her lying alone waiting for the police. I had a connection with her in the same way I had a connection with my mother when she used to read and sing to me. Take off the Burberry costume and they were one and the same to me."

"Not quite." My father squeezes my hand harder and then brushes a stray hair from my face. "You said there were two things?"

"I missed the second thing at first. It wasn't until I was thinking about families and the charts Jess had done that it dawned on me Carolyn went by her mother's name." My father frowns in confusion. "On your chart," I explain, "Jess had your name linked to Charlotte Harper with me as your joint offspring. On the chart Jess started for Carolyn, she drew a line between Deborah *Holt* and Carolyn's name as mother and daughter. Jess hadn't finished filling in the marital connection and line between Carolyn and her parents. She only had notated an *H* in the slot for Carolyn's father. Apparently, although she felt her research was correct, Jess wanted to confirm why Carolyn didn't use her father's Harper name so that she could annotate the chart accordingly."

"And that frightened Carolyn?" My father releases my hand as he uses both to gesture with.

"I think so. When Jess questioned Carolyn to confirm her father's real last name was Harper, not Holt, Carolyn concluded everyone at Sunshine Village would soon know her secret. By killing Jess with the bees, she thought she could keep anyone from finding out her true parentage. She would have succeeded if my mother had never come back to see us."

I ask my father to hand me the well-worn copy of *Goodnight Moon* I clutched all the way to the hospital and that now sits on my hospital nightstand. I take it from him with my unencumbered hand. "Do you know what's so important about this copy of *Goodnight Moon*?" I hold the book so he can see it, too. "Why Carolyn wanted it so badly?"

We can both see from its spine that the book has been read often, but the book's covers are in pristine condition.

"I don't know. When you were little, it was your favorite book. I remember your mother reading it to you over and over. Funny, I don't remember reading it to you after your mother left."

Not only don't I remember him reading it to me after my mother left, I don't remember seeing it again until the day my mother was killed. "When Charlotte came to see you, Dad, did she bring you this copy of *Goodnight Moon*?"

He thinks for a moment. "She must have. I brought only a few books to Sunshine Village from home, and surely you or I would have noticed it when we set up my bookcase."

My father is right. We carefully selected which books to bring to Sunshine Village. I kept some books from his personal library, and through Carolyn we donated the remainder to the Wahoo Library. If he'd had this copy of *Goodnight Moon,* one of the three of us would have seen it. If it had been Carolyn, she would have destroyed it then.

With my one hand, I flip the book open to the title page. Memories of *Goodnight Moon*'s simple story and my mother's voice come back to me. To avoid bursting into tears, I think of the Halloween afternoon when Molly was reading the book to him. She told me then she read it because he kept holding it out to her and repeating the words: "Read, Carrie." I had assumed my father was so agitated that her choice of this book was what calmed him down. Now I realize that in his mental state he wanted me to read it because my mother had brought the book back to me.

I read aloud the beautifully penned inscription on the title page: "To my first niece—May you share my love of words and books. Aunt Carolyn."

My father lets out a sigh. "If I only knew . . ."

"Dad, the reality is that until I realized Carolyn Holt used her mother's name, instead of her birth name, Brian and I never linked Carolyn to the vandalism of my car and Lindy's death. Once the facts were laid out, it made perfect sense."

I pause to take a sip of water. "Like me, Carolyn thought the letter was written by my mother. Just as she was afraid the *Goodnight Moon* book would give her away, she was scared the letter mentioned the half-sister relationship between my mother and her. When she learned I hadn't read it and it was in my glove compartment, she knew she had a very small window of time before Brian and I opened it. Once Marta chased us all out of her room, she had to go for it. Lindy had the bad luck of starting her constitutional when Carolyn was breaking into my car."

"But your car was in the parking lot, not on the Riverwalk." My father rubs his brow.

"True, but Carolyn only saw Lindy leaving the building and looking around. She didn't realize Lindy had tunnel vision only for the Riverwalk and probably never even glanced in the direction of the parking lot. I firmly believe Lindy would have gone back into the building or screamed if she had seen Carolyn breaking into my car."

"You're right. Lindy wouldn't have been quiet." My father smiles as do I.

"Anyway, after pushing Lindy, Carolyn covered her tracks by going to the main desk and pretending she unsuccessfully tried calling the nursing station to report the alarm."

I let the book close, secure that, despite the horrible choice my mother made thinking she was protecting my father and me, she kept this copy of *Goodnight Moon* all these years because she cherished me. I also think about how many people my aunt hurt to keep me from finding out my true heritage or her role in changing my life. Before I close my eyes again, I reach for my father's hand while glancing at the flowers and balloons. I drift away, comfortable today in my father's love and knowing that, even if they aren't related to me, there are people out there who care about me like family.

ABOUT THE AUTHOR

Debra H. Goldstein has been described as a judge, author, litigator, wife, step-mom, mother of twins, civic volunteer, and loyal University of Michigan alumna. *Maze in Blue,* her debut novel, received a 2012 Independent Book Publisher (IPPY) Award and was reissued as a May 2014 selection by Harlequin Worldwide Mysteries. Her short stories and non-fiction essays include *Thanksgiving in Moderation, Who Dat? Dat the Indian Chief!, Legal Magic, Malicious Mischief, Grandma's Garden, The Rabbi's Wife Stayed Home,* and *Maybe I Should Hug You.*

Judge Goldstein lives in Alabama, with her husband, whose blood runs crimson.